with warmest wishes,

Roy

FATTY GOES
TO CHINA

Oct 2012

FATTY GOES TO CHINA

TO CHINA

Royston Tester

Tightrope Books
17 Greyton Crescent
Toronto, Ontario. M6E 2G1
www.tightropebooks.com

Edited: Carolina Smart
Author photograph: Dale Koe
Cover art: Zhang Xiaogang
Cover design: David Bingham
Typography: Dawn Kresan
Printed and bound in Canada

We thank the Canada Council for the Arts and the Ontario Arts Council
for their support of our publishing program.

Canada Council   Conseil des Arts   ONTARIO ARTS COUNCIL
for the Arts   du Canada   CONSEIL DES ARTS DE L'ONTARIO

Library and Archives Canada Cataloguing in Publication

Tester, Royston Mark
    Fatty goes to China / Royston Tester.

Short stories.
ISBN 978-1-926639-48-2

    I. TITLE.

PS8639.E88F38 2012   C813'.6   C2012-901807-4

for Lei

TABLE OF CONTENTS

FOUR GENTLEMEN AND
A COMFORT WOMAN

At the end of August as Zhang Xiaoya turned into a duck, or believed so, her revered grandmother's print above the radiator began to moan. Nightly. Winter plum blossom on a craggy headland, pen and ink, all sniffs and sobbing.

At first Zhang Xiaoya took no notice.

Truth was, the career opportunity at Da Dong, Beijing's Finest Duck Restaurant, was wearing thin. Assisting an army of bawdy carvers—"Ho-hum Yaya, what golden tits tonight"—the twenty-five year old arranged a head, skin and buff breasts upon on a platter. I live in duck, she would tell herself, exasperated. Poultry moonscape, six days out of seven. Hefty shifts, wages pity-little. No wonder I can't sleep.

Yesterday, she gobbed five times into Da Dong's signature soup. How can I do better? She spat. Earn more for my mother who's visiting on Thursday? Find a boyfriend? Honour my grandmother? Another lickety spit. How do I overcome duck?

At the Tuanjiehu apartment, Zhang Xiaoya ogled a hand-held mirror and felt pockmarked. Flesh too drawn. Was it Beijing air? Nose and mouth rather amiably pulled back. Too Japanese, eyes too small. Spiny fingers! Were they always so…webbed?

"How long have you been a duck?" she asked herself, pretending for China Central Television, English edition. Not even her roommates cared.

"It began with the Summer Olympics," Zhang Xiaoya replied, adjusting a red-thread jade anklet. "I imagined taking the hurdles differently."

She dared not look into her eye. Ringed. Speck of gold in its pupil.

"Three of us are trainee chefs," she said, as though it had once been inspiring. "Drummed out of Nanjing Foreign Languages Institute."

Zhang Xiaoya watched her five sleeping co-workers—all fellow migrants, one an Evian Mineral Water Maid from Wuhan—more fatigued than she. On their bunk-beds, trussed up in summer coverlets, cellphones blinking at the pillow.

Before she could resume her international power-interview, she again heard the Caucasian weeping from next door. Zhang Xiaoya turned to her grandmother's *Plum Blossom* drawing. She lifted her heel from the radiator. Black dust footprint upon the cooling ribs.

"It's only plum blossom dew," she told the mirror, moistening her eyes for effect. "Landing in our sitting-room."

Tomorrow, Zhang Xiaoya would perform a duty toward the unhappy, older woman seeping into the grey-walled quarters.

"Duck on a mission," she told the phantom interviewer. "Will this be a global documentary, CCTV9?"

Zhang Xiaoya felt sorry for the Canadian visitor who was living in the apartment beside hers. No residence permit, tourist visa run out, most likely. Beijing Public Security could be merciless to expiring aliens. Ruthie Nolan was obviously one of those Olympic visitors. In her early sixties, overstaying her welcome, sketching relentlessly in the yard—a canyon of tower blocks on every side. The woman drew idealized Chinese landscapes, *guo hua*, neither she nor anyone ever witnessed 'for real.' Every brushstroke, a reckless first and last. No going over, ever. How come this foreigner mastered it?

"Zhang Xiaoya, and China, we should play proper host," the young woman said. Tuanjiehu neighbours were too courteous and reserved about Westerners. "There are so many tears from 403."

Zhang Xiaoya would not be discrete at all. She was Plum Blossom's "very un-Chinese" a granddaughter, of impure race. Zhang Xiaoya's widowed mother frequently lamented as much. "You're a half-caste, my child. Is this why you're cheeky? Where's your modesty?"

Canada would melt with joy at the intrusion of a local. The Ruthie Nolans of this world knew nothing of 'China versus Japan.' How can I go wrong, thought Zhang Xiaoya? Beady-eyed fowl in the making, I can do business with any sorry foreigner. I can overcome duck.

We women, fast friends for life.

"The best samples from your portfolio, please," Zhang Xiaoya said as she cleared a space on the sofa, junction of nine crossroads, in Ruthie Nolan's vacation apartment. The young woman settled beside a Nasca pizza box and jar of cottonseed. The room was cluttered with mulberry paper, and there was a stench of pinewood-soot and glue. A rack of brushes stood upon a floor cushion, ink pots here and there, drawings. An open suitcase, swollen with clothes, sat in the centre of the room. A Beijing subway map lay abandoned in its folds, a bottle of 'Dexamethasone.'

Ruthie nodded quickly, sorting with her left hand.

"My boss is very particular about the interior of Da Dong restaurant."

"Of course."

The white-haired lady, evidently unaccustomed to visitors or to selling paintings to a restaurant flitted—was that a limp?—about the room. She bundled rolls of 'double shuen' paper onto a stove. Gathered her art as though reeling in carp: *Summer Bamboo, Spring Orchid, Cliff-top Village, Winding Tracks.* She held up *Forests Dotted Upon a Hump-Backed Hill* and pulled a face.

Ruthie made the visitor nervous.

"Beautiful," muttered Zhang Xiaoya, pocketing a one hundred yuan note that had slipped to the floor. I should never have done that, she thought. Zhang Xiaoya gazed at black strokes—from bold 'charred' stems, branches and rocky outcrops, to light-grey rivers and a waterfall. "You paint with the left hand?" She noted Ruthie's right arm hanging uselessly.

"It's been my hobby for years," the elderly woman said. "I'm a secretary, really."

13

"The bonework's strong." Zhang Xiaoya pointed to a chrysanthemum, and forgot about the banknote. "Delicate petals."

"Yes?" Ruthie put a hand to her mouth. Zhang Xiaoya noticed the wedding ring buried in swollen knuckle.

"My grandmother's name was Plum Blossom," Zhang Xiaoya said, suspecting Ruthie was ill. "There's a *Plum Blossom* namesake picture, not as good as yours here, on my apartment wall."

What was wrong, wondered Zhang Xiaoya? The foreigner let out a whimper, and steadied herself against the bookshelf. Eyes squinty with anticipation.

"Plum Blossom and my mother Xiu are arriving from Shanghai this Thursday afternoon," the young woman added, rather too decisively. "I'm taking the whole day off."

"Great," from behind the Canadian fingers. Ruthie leaned on the glass-fronted cabinet. It rattled.

"I'll show my boss *all* your flowers," Zhang Xiaoya said, thrusting scrolls and a sealed yellow envelope into her shopping bag. She looked ahead, duck on a mission, flushed with embarrassment that this precarious lady might collapse. Or was nuts. Ruthie Nolan might not last a week!

"I'm going to rest," Ruthie said. The Westerner had reached limits of her own.

"Today, you're like a three-inch golden lotus," Zhang Xiaoya told Ruthie in the foreigner's apartment next evening. She conveyed a Da Dong request for more samples—although Zhang Xiaoya had yet to deliver the previous batch to her employer. "Bound feet like Plum Blossom's, the size of a cigarette packet."

"What do you mean?"

"'Nei jin wai song,'" Zhang Xiaoya said, noticing some heavy-handed doodling on a notepad beside the phone. "'Tense within but relaxed without.'"

"'内紧外松?'" Ruthie repeated. "That's me, you think?"

"Just like my grandmother's feet in Nanjing, yes."

Zhang Xiaoya described a plump, white stockinged instep, crammed into dainty red shoes, as though the owner were a Disney doe.

"Can Plum Blossom walk?"

"Little girl steps," said Zhang Xiaoya, zig-zagging about the room.

"Men thought it attractive?"

"Tiny lips too," she giggled. "Like you've sipped vinegar."

"Hm."

"These doodles are not *guo hua*," Zhang Xiaoya said, halting at Ruthie's phone. Doodles? A tree growing inside someone's house, cords of alphabet spiralling into black sky….'THE TERMINATOR' scribbled down one side."

"Phone calls from home," Ruthie explained. "A pine tree fell onto my house and went through the living-room window."

"That's awful."

"My friend's taking care of it," Ruthie said. "Plus the mail I forgot to stop and a cracked street-main that flooded the rockery and my basement."

"Wow," said Zhang Xiaoya. "In Toronto?"

"One thing after another."

"Did you leave Canada in a rush?"

"I wanted to see the Olympics."

"Alone?" Zhang Xiaoya envied Westerners' freedoms.

"No-one else could come."

"Have you forgotten to go home?"

Ruthie glared at her.

"*Guo hua* drawings like yours saved my grandmother's life," Zhang Xiaoya said, undeterred.

"Is that so?"

Foreigners were kids before an ancient Chinese story. You could tell them anything, really. Fairy tales will inspire more paintings for Da Dong, thought Zhang Xiaoya. Cheer the old lady up.

"At sixteen, Plum Blossom was forced to be a comfort woman for the Japanese who invaded our hometown," she told Ruthie whose attention seemed to falter. "Many soldiers found bare, crushed feet ugly and the officers were going to kill my grandmother before she was fully used."

Ruthie reached for a teapot. "Some men would find the smell of rotting feet a turn-on, don't you think?"

Zhang Xiaoya collected herself. "One of the American missionaries smuggled Plum Blossom out of Nanjing to Shanghai," she went on, sorting Ruthie's paintings. "Eventually there was a ship to the United States."

"One of the *fortunate* women," said Ruthie, as though playing along.

Enthralled by Ruthie's odd manners, Zhang Xiaoya leafed through another folder. Ruthie poured tea at a clip.

"Everything was arranged using carrier-pigeons," Zhang Xiaoya told her, resuming the narrative. "With coded directions written into miniature *guo hua* sketches like yours."

"The Japanese intercepted them, surely?"

"Often." Zhang Xiaoya chose *Summer Bamboo* from the Westerner's portfolio. It was her mother Xiu's namesake plant. "In the drawings, the information was all wrong except in a region of woodland on one of the mountains."

"They wrote secret messages into that part?"

"Trees and other tiny brushstrokes for numbers in a map reference," Zhang Xiaoya said, more urgently than she wished. "Sent several times a day to our forces inland."

"The Japanese couldn't shoot all the birds, I imagine."

Ruthie planted a cup in the young woman's hand.

"They were busy burying Chinese people alive or using them for bayonet practice," Zhang Xiaoya told her. "Instead of opening a capsule on some pigeon's leg."

"Plum Blossom went through a terrible ordeal."

"Nanjing's history is with me."

Zhang Xiaoya paused. Storytelling about her grandmother, to this particular audience, was more difficult than she anticipated. Ruthie Nolan was utterly unshockable.

"I'm sorry," said Ruthie. She moved closer to Zhang Xiaoya. "It's difficult telling tales, isn't it?"

"Westerners often know more about our Japanese massacres, and Chinese comfort women, than we do." Zhang Xiaoya's voice was tight.

Ruthie contemplated her. "Are you going to rob me again this evening, by the way?"

"Pardon?" Zhang Xiaoya peered into the blue of Ruthie's eyes. "That hundred yuan note."

"You must be mistaken."

Ruthie shook her head.

Zhang Xiaoya foraged beneath the sofa for more paintings. She had forgotten about the note. Who would ask a question like that, she wondered? "I found you a new client at Da Dong restaurant."

"That's not the point, is it?"

"You're mistaken."

Ruthie opened the front door. "Please stay away from me, Zhang Xiaoya."

A Canadian's three-inch golden lotus sharply up the Nanjing backside.

Early Thursday morning, Zhang Xiaoya savoured a rare sleep-in. Her roommates snickered and fussed more noisily than usual.

Later, the doorbell rang.

In tea-coloured flip-flops and silk pyjamas, she shuffled from her bunk.

"Still a duck?" said Ruthie Nolan standing tall, in skirt and polished shoes.

"Waw," Zhang Xiaoya muttered, gripping her hair into a tortoiseshell comb. "Time out."

"Your mother arrives today."

Zhang Xiaoya nodded—feeling alarm that Ruthie might wish to meet her.

"I've come to say goodbye," Ruthie said. "I brought you this." She handed the young woman a scroll.

Zhang Xiaoya smelled its freshness. "You're returning to Toronto?"

"No," she replied. "Open it, please."

It was a drawing of spring orchids on hilly land. A scarlet seal in its corner, recently pressed with cinnabar paste.

"My namesake flower," Zhang Xiaoya said. "Now I have all *Four Gentlemen* of yours."

"Oh?" replied Ruthie. She glanced into the room.

Zhang Xiaoya smiled. "*Autumn Chrysanthemum, Summer Bamboo, Winter Plum Blossom* and *this*."

"They're called *Four Gentlemen*?"

As Zhang Xiaoya unravelled the paper, she examined her friend's script aside the carefully placed stamp.

"Does the Mandarin read properly?" Ruthie said.

Zhang Xiaoya raised the painting high. "'A quiet spot, deep within the mountains.'"

"It saved your grandmother, didn't you say? This style? The coded strokes?"

"Why don't you come inside, Ruthie?"

She hesitated. "I'm on the way to a clinic."

"You are sick?" A subject Zhang Xiaoya wished to evade.

Ruthie bowed slightly. "Did you pick up a yellow envelope, by mistake, the other night?"

"I did," said Zhang Xiaoya . "Along with the portfolio."

Ruthie followed her into the sitting-room.

"Don't mind our Evian Maid bottle," Zhang Xiaoya said, referring to the seven-foot standup poster for a mineral water, with grinning face aloft, and white cardboard arms outstretched near the window.

"Evian!"

"Your envelope's been opened," Zhang Xiaoya told her.

Ruthie crept toward blue French Alps in the cardboard cut-out.

"How did that happen?" Zhang Xiaoya wondered, handing over the empty packet.

"*You* tell *me*," said Ruthie, face to face with Evian's peaks. A handful of X-rays taped to the Maid's head.

"Oh no."

"Quite a party."

Ruthie was transfixed by the images, spread like a peacock's tail.

"X-rays," Zhang Xiaoya said. "In colour."

The shimmering fan of galaxies, bronze and green. A hundred yuan note in its plumage.

"My crazy roomies, did it."

Ruthie stopped her hand. The two women—three, with Evian—looked at one another.

"These are shots of your head, Ruthie?"

Toronto's face a blizzard.

"I could kill those jokers," said Zhang Xiaoya. "What were they thinking?"

"It's okay," Ruthie told her. "There's my hundred, I guess."

"I'll take the X-rays down."

"See that tiny circle?" said Ruthie, pointing to an incongruous, ringed sun in a turquoise valley. "A few more weeks, I'm afraid."

Zhang Xiaoya held Ruthie's left arm.

"My doctor calls it 'The Terminator.'"

"Oh."

"Such a comedian."

"What should I do, Ruthie?"

"There's nothing, dear," she replied. "No carrier pigeon's going to beat a Terminator."

Zhang Xiaoya looked in horror at the skulls. "So you've run away?"

"I came to the Olympics to make a strategy."

"This is it?" asked Zhang Xiaoya, leading Ruthie to a blue plastic chair.

"Let's call it the grandmother moment."

"You have grandchildren?" said Zhang Xiaoya.

"No children," she replied Ruthie, sitting. "I was thinking of Plum Blossom. Your *grandmother*." She indicated the namesake print above the radiator.

"What about her?"

"She's not coming with your mother Xiu this afternoon, is she?"

Zhang Xiaoya studied heads, a sun, the Alps of a mineral bottle.

"Not alive, right? Never made it to America?"

What was there to lose…to a death row-er? How smart this Westerner thinks she is, thought Zhang Xiaoya. "Plum Blossom died in Nanjing."

"You shouldn't look so sadly at *Four Gentlemen*."

"I misled you."

"It was a hunch," said Ruthie.

"In 1938, giving birth to my mother, is when Plum Blossom died."

Ruthie perused the Evian summits, nerve and bone.

"My grandfather is Japanese," Zhang Xiaoya said sadly. She looked at the X-rays. "I'm not used to saying."

"I figured."

"One of the soldiers did it."

Ridges, gorges, red lettering—on the Maid and inside Ruthie's head. "*Xiao Riben*, they call me at Da Dong," she went on. "Little Japanese!"

"Your roommates too?"

Zhang Xiaoya nodded. "My features give it away," she said. "Yet my father was from Shanghai."

For several minutes, the two women sat silently before Evian.

"I've snuck away from my family," Ruthie said eventually. She climbed to her feet. "From that 'friend,' who is my husband."

"They know nothing?"

"Not a dickie bird." Ruth corralled her heads and slipped them into the envelope. "I want it like that."

"You do?" said Zhang Xiaoya, terrified for this woman who had run away. She looked at Evian's three peaks. Rising like a dragon from swirling pink sea. "Come with me to the railway station."

Zhang Xiaoya stood.

Recklessly, the women sought paths before a deep-set mountain.

"Your mother Xiu will be overjoyed to see you." With her one good arm, she embraced Zhang Xiaoya. The yellow envelope in Ruthie's hand creased at the young woman's back.

"I'm not a little girl," Ruthie said.

"Neither am I," whispered Zhang Xiaoya, turning her around. "I insist you come and meet Xiu from the Shanghai train."

"Why would I want to do that?"

"Xiu's not always overjoyed to see me."

Ruthie stared at the packet of X-rays. "You need reinforcements?"

Zhang Xiaoya teased the envelope from her friend's fingers. "Tense within but relaxed without."

Ruthie rolled her eyes. "Let's leave it on that chair."

No going over.

"There." Zhang Xiaoya said, patting its golden face square.

Ever.

QUEENS TAKE LONGER, I SUPPOSE

"They know how much depends on particulars—the
particular wrong answer, the particular bowl of soup, the
strength of a particular pair of lungs."

—John Berger, *A Painter of our Time*

Emil's visit to Weimar earlier this year had shaken him up.

Along Clinton Street in December drizzle, he scooped a leaf from the sidewalk. Doesn't it just have to be beech? Warm to the touch, like skin. Emil turned its tiny stalk.

The story of the Rileys does not really begin or end with a beech leaf, or with Weimar, Germany—but he had to grab onto something. There was precious else.

He walked past the Diplomatico restaurant in Toronto's 'Little Italy,' sliding his thumb over the leaf's glossy, bronze cheek. He felt ridiculous at behaving so harshly towards his friends.

On College Street, he looked back at the Rileys' car reversing into the one-way Clinton. Barry's amused expression through the half-open tinted window, scoffing at his wife's driving. Linda's teary eyes. Her tattooed arm struggling to turn the wheel.

She was not upset about maneuvering their obstinate Renault from the school parking lot. Emil knew it was their fruitless afternoon—where nothing had been regained in friendship.

"Are you wasting time eating with us?" Barry had said. "You're too much work, Emil Benedetti-Toc."

Linda had been enraged at their friend's conduct.

Wave, man, Emil told himself. The three of you have been close for a decade. You can do more than craft wood, you freak of a journeyman. You should make up with the likes of Barry and Linda Riley.

Emil stood at the corner. You're enjoying the cruelty, said a voice in his head. You should stop.

At the meal with Barry and Linda, Emil had related an incident that dominated his holiday: the news of his brother Adrian's attack on Christiane Bucur, a mutual friend.

"Opinel knife blade," Christiane had informed Emil on the telephone. "It's like you're butter."

The incident in Berlin—a city hall department party, a depressed Adrian Benedetti-Toc—left the young woman paralyzed. In Emil's many calls, he had been moved, though not surprised, by Christiane's will to overcome that setback, by her concern for the assailant.

From the Mitte Clinic, Christiane tried to understand Adrian's mental state, and the effect of his imprisonment on his wife Helga and their children, whom Christiane knew. The effect on Emil and his younger brother Paolo.

"Feeling some heel and toe today," she said. "Much more sensation."

Emil imagined the creeping back.

He pictured the family around the bed. Gisela and Magdalena consoling their mother, and Norbert's hands upon her flesh. Her two daughters brushing Christiane's hair. Norbert massaging the feet, rolling brightly coloured socks onto them. Running his hands along her arms, around the fingertips.

"Norbert's very good," Christiane told Emil. "You must find a devotee like him."

"I think of spring, Emil," Christiane said. "Your return to Viscri. So many visits these days! Just imagine how often you can come to Berlin, tour my office at the Rotesrathaus. You'll need vacations from the Prince of Wales contract."

By March, and Emil's visit, surely she will stand?

Through Christmas and New Year, Emil looked forward to spring. Greenery, regeneration. A pair of new shoes on Christiane's feet.

"She may never walk properly," Emil said to Barry and Linda. "But she will get about somehow. Return to her Rathaustrasse job, with faculties intact."

"I'm pleased she survived, Emil."

Barry agreed.

"Amazing she'd worry about the murderer, huh?" Linda added, nose in the menu.

"He wasn't a murderer," Barry said.

"*Attempted* murderer," she replied, pointing at one of the 'Specials.'

Emil failed to mention his brother Adrian's role. He thought it might frighten the Rileys, as it had scared him. Adrian always was a firebrand capable of going too far.

"I accepted a deal with the Prince of Wales," Emil told them, once they had ordered food.

"Congratulations."

"How did *that* happen?" Linda asked.

"He's renovating his property in my village, Viscri," said Emil. "He offered me the commission."

"Nice one," Linda said. She looked mortified.

Emil wondered what else to tell them.

"It was my sister's turn to do the turkey this Christmas, Emil," Linda said. "Sandra might be a social worker, but our family winds her up, you know. Too country, most of 'em, for her liking."

After the last mince pies were eaten, brandies chugged—"and without laying a finger on the dishes"—Linda's sister went to the new 'King Kong' film, near Brampton Mall. "Sandra was the only one in the cinema!"

"Goofball sister," Barry said.

"She hadn't realized how deep the plot was," Linda went on, encouraged. "The movie's set in the Great Depression, 1930s."

Like a sparrow, Barry nibbled squares of bread. He glanced at a streetcar.

Emil looked at him, frustrated that this man had become such a stranger. Remote. So perverse in betraying him last year when Emil was away in his Transylvania hometown.

Barry had tried unsuccessfully to introduce Fernando and Ios to one another. They were two of Emil's former, longtime lovers. What was Barry about? *Schadenfreude*? The man had a taste for stirring trouble. He could never quite ignore Emil's loves.

"My sister got completely involved in the movie," Linda said. "How Anne Darrow, the unemployed vaudeville actress, is picked up on the streets of Manhattan for an expedition to some uncharted Skull Island in Sumatra."

"*Uncharted?*"

"You heard."

"Read that, did you?" he asked. "I thought Sandra went to see Adrian Brody? Isn't he in it?"

"That too."

"How does Anne Darrow love a King Kong, then?" said Emil.

"By dancing for him," replied Linda. "Juggling and doing somersaults."

"Wild time in the sack?" Barry dropped his jaw for more bread. Linda jabbed him.

At the end of 'King Kong,' after the ape falls to his death from the Empire State Building, Linda's sister sat in the auditorium. A teenaged usher, in a black blazer, by the exit.

"That good?" said Barry. "Or was Sandra petrified by rampaging T-Rexes and giant spiders?"

"It's a 'Beauty and the Beast' knock-off, isn't it?" Emil asked.

The usher came up to Linda's sister and asked if she was okay.

"'I'm not a loser,' Sandra told the girl. 'Here all by myself.' The usher looked at my sister. 'As though I'm retarded.' 'All my company's gone,' Sandra told the black blazer. 'I needed to chill.'"

Barry laughed. "It's the sisters' greatest fear, Emil," he said. "To be solitary and have someone notice."

"Sitting alone with King Kong must be tough."

"You guys," said Linda. "My sister was *embarrassed*. Alone on Christmas Day like a leper? C'mon! It's not Sandra one bit."

Emil wanted to forgive Barry for his devious conduct while he was overseas. The crime was not so heinous. Why was Emil swept up in so much revulsion? A tide that would not recede. Had he once harboured feelings for Barry? Maybe so. Emil had not spoken to his work colleague for months, nor to Linda. He had declined an invitation for Thanksgiving. It was like being paralyzed.

Emil stood at the corner, beside the Diplomatico, and watched as the Rileys' car made its way north to Harbord Street, brake lights flickering. In goodbye, he hoped.

You're a pathetic Romanian immigrant Emil Toc, he told himself. Feeling exploited and betrayed at every turn. You hold resentment, like a flame, to your breast. Smarten up, as Linn would say. You've grown fat on Canada.

At Emil's Parkdale apartment above the laundromat, Linn was sprawled on a couch.

"Survived the Rileys?" he asked, pinching Emil's arm.

Linn had let himself in. He was bouncing Seriously, their green and yellow speckled monkey (a teddy-monkey, to be frank), on his knee.

"What do you think?"

"You dumped them?" Linn said, wiggling Seriously's arms in a sing-song. "Using you for thrills again, were they?"

Emil lay against Linn's thigh.

Affectionately, Linn began to twist his hair and pluck at imaginary knots. "No."

"You can't?" He yanked a clump of thick, black hair. "Or won't?"

"It's not the answer," Emil said.

Linn pulled once, twice. The roots tenting like gooseflesh. "What is the answer?"

"Got me there, Linn." He wrenched his head free, and took the tan leaf from his pocket. Emil laid it in his palm.

"Flora indoors?" Linn asked, recoiling.

"Toss it?"

"Leaves are full of germs, don't you know that?"

Emil placed his find on a side table—beneath a mantelpiece that held lollipop-stick models of tables, chairs, and a Transylvania four-poster bed. He was determined the leaf would mean something. "I'm hanging onto it."

The leaf felt drier in the house. Its many veins prominent and losing lustre.

"I don't want the Rileys as friends," Emil said. "I don't get them anymore."

"Very revealing, Emil."

"That I'm fucked in the head?"

"About friendship," he shot back. "You don't know much."

There was always skin, witness Bachalowsky reported at the Nuremberg trials. They skinned prisoners, then tanned the skin. Emil stares at an exhibit board in Buchenwald camp, near Weimar.

It is January 3rd, 2005.

He has taken a break from the year's leave to Viscri. Emil is visiting his childhood friend Christiane in Germany. They have travelled south from Berlin to stay with her husband Norbert's parents and to enjoy the famous city of Goethe, Schiller, and Bach.

Emil is chilled to the bone.

The group spends the morning on a hike to the Etter Keep. The panorama of rolling hills delights Emil. A trail through the beech wood entices the visitors along. Hitler's S.S., a note explains, received orders for human flesh. It was also given, as gifts, to Buchenwald's staff and visitors. To be used as book covers, lampshades, and gloves.

Emil gazes at the sentence—*You are here.* He is standing where the pre-skinned stood. He is walking their paths, admiring the same distant fields, trees, and sky. Winds tear up the Ettersberg mountain. A pallid, winter sun gives no heat.

'Buchenwald' means beech wood, Emil reads. He wonders whether translation matters.

"Everyone should visit the camp," Christiane's husband says. "Observe how well we Germans bite our nails."

"He doesn't have to, Norbert."

"Don't I?"

They need to move.

You do not drop in on a concentration camp.

Norbert and Christiane pass through the entrance with its cynical, iron wrought dictum: *Jedem Das Seine* ('To Each According to his Merits').

Beyond, there is nothing but a giant space on the hillside. Wind, silence. Beech trees, oak and birch far off. Evergreen. Barbed wire.

A parade ground? Devil's footprint?

After that, on closer inspection, stand the foundations— some recognized with carefully placed stones, recently lain flowers—of buildings. Where prisoners were housed.

Human tattooed skin was piled in Block 2. Nazis were especially fascinated by tattoos with obscene images.

He is standing in front of a roped area. A mound of ordinary footwear within. One particular shoe after another. Inmates were here for years, or hours or forever. Two hundred and fifty thousand men, women. Wrong answers, and bowls of soup. Children in Block 66.

Emil lasts forty-five minutes. Christiane and Norbert hurry with him up the slope towards the gate. No-one speaks. *Jedem Das Seine.* The three bent forward. A Thuringian gale whips leaves and twigs across their shins.

Emil's cheek is wet from cold, eyes stinging. A New Year. Difficult to know if you're weeping—in such pain to flee.

Waiting for a ride into Weimar. Emil mouths the line.

Or would you call a cab? We're at Buchenwald. You can't miss it. There's a chimney. Ornamental gatework and so on. Summary executions. Medical experiments.

Goethe never stood here. Or Schiller, Bach. At the end of …. What's the name of this street? Emil looks across the road. Sign as bold as day: *Blut Strasse.* Couldn't be anything but blood.

Or did he? Where would Goethe have strolled, before death camps? Might he have walked between these trees? Sat beneath a beech on the Ettersberg mountain. Praising heaven for his triumphant *Sorrows of Young Werther*? Mumbling phrases that would become *Faust*?

Not the embarrassed hush of Emil, Christiane and Norbert. His was a pause between verses and imagining. Theirs was shame.

"Here's the bus," says Christiane. She points down the hill.

"People knew," says Norbert, lifting his packsack.

Emil glances at the beech tree alongside. Its ribs sparring.

"Pedestrians watched road gangs from the camp," Norbert goes on. "At the munitions factory, Weimar labourers worked next to starving Buchenwald prisoners."

In Viscri, Emil is using beech for the royal four-posters. He presses his hand against its smooth, silver-grey belly. Carved initials, like a beard. In summer, the dense twiggery and foliage would obscure any sun. In Romania, they call it 'the mosaic tree.' Leaves splayed alternately on a branch, like scattered pages. A kaleidoscope for anyone below.

This afternoon, the tree's elbowing its way from winter.

Christiane boards the bus.

Emil looks at Norbert's back. Local citizens knew about Buchenwald but not the details. Like a burgher, Emil says nothing. Buys the ticket, finds his bones a place.

Journey into Weimar—fifteen minutes.

Linn had brought his rice cooker and was in the kitchen preparing a dinner of eggplant and steamed vegetables. Emil had his dried beech leaf for company, and Seriously. The Riley rigmarole to disentangle. Stay or go? You'd think an immigrant would know.

Linn was unequivocal about friends like these. He made meals after the direst pronouncements. The man Emil loved, grappling with a rice cooker.

His name—Linn—bemused Emil. It meant 'sensitive plant.' There he was advocating the breaking of ties with Linda and Barry. "At least it's a solution." Pale flowers without petals, only pistils, was a Linn. Thorns on its red-brown stems.

What Emil liked about 'sensitive plant Linn' was that in its native country, where rainfall was merciless, a drop of water, or any touch, would cause the fern-like leaves to close, decisively, and so protect the tender fronds inside.

"Go to her," Linn said immediately, on hearing of Christiane's stabbing.

"Cut them off!" he declared of the Rileys, learning about Barry's lover-mongering. "The guy's a closet-case, right?"

When Emil divined that Christiane would live, and that she needed respite, he arranged to see her on his return to Europe in a fortnight's time. A visit he would parlay, with his boss Mr. Diewick's approval, into five months between Berlin and Viscri—to complete his princely beds. He would take Seriously with him.

"Another trip!" Christiane said.

The Linn plant is poisonous. It is also a herb to calm people, and arrest bleeding. Maybe that was the part of him in Emil's kitchen. Just as Emil had not flown instantly to Berlin, so he would not eliminate the Rileys from his life. This was where Emil was headed, he now understood. He would keep company with people who betrayed him.

How King-Kong.

Barry requested the lunchtime tab.

"My husband's in the money, aren't you darlin'?"

Linda hugged him.

"You've seen his flyers, Emil?"

She reached into her handbag and brought out a leaflet. "Pile, pack or perch on it. Palette is a multi-purpose furniture module that serves as seat, shelf or table. $189.99."

"We've got clients," Linda told him.

"Can't be journeymen forever, can we, Emil?"

"Not at all."

At Diewick's Furniture Systems, Barry and Emil built mail-flow stations, vertical dividers with stop dado joints. Melamine interiors, finished backs, wall mounted or stacked. A living you could sleepwalk.

"That explains the gold?" said Emil, indicating Linda's fingers and thumb. Each ringed.

Her eyes teared up. "I took Barry to the mall to show him the jewellery I liked," she said, gravely. "All different styles and price ranges."

"Wanting to be fair," Barry explained, frowning at the restaurant bill.

"Christmas morning, I open my gifts," Linda said, proffering her hands for Emil.

"All your choices?"

"Every one!" Linda unbuttoned her blouse. "This too." A seagull on a glittering chain, imperial jade, upon a rosy cleavage.

"Beautiful."

"Barry's my man, ain't y'love?"

He looked across at Emil. "I owed her big time," Barry said. "After that dinner I set up with your two ex-boyfriends."

"I was mad with him," Linda told Emil. "Sandra gave him a right bollocking too. 'What will Emil think?' she kept saying."

"You didn't tell me that."

"We never see you, Emil!" she scolded. "We wanted to face off like this, clear the air."

It had taken Emil months.

"You wouldn't meet," Barry said. "Or *talk*."

"After such an insult?"

"My husband pokes his pecker in all the wrong places," Linda said. "You know that. There's an Irish leprechaun in him."

"I'm sorry." Barry held out his palm.

"Make him pay with rings, Emil."

Linda re-admired her collection.

Emil stood up. "Let's be going." How Canadian-couch an apology, he thought. Cuts no quarter with me. "Everything's a joke to you," he told them. Easy, trite, and suffering-free.

"What do you mean?" said Barry.

"I'm not a toy," Emil told them. "You need to pay attention to what you do."

"Who do you think you are?" Linda said, pushing past Emil to the terrace. "You don't deserve friends."

Emil followed her onto College Street. He felt a hand on his shoulder. "Any chance of a nip of whisky at your place?" asked Barry. "Delicious pastry to finish off?"

His friendship had begun with Barry—and became more about Linda. He and Barry used to talk carpentry, exhibitions. The two men dreamt up Diewick trade missions to London's Hoxton neighbourhood to see new 'Brit-art.' Barry had disappeared into his wife. No world his old mate wished to explore.

"Where did you park your car?" Emil asked. "I'll walk with you."

"We might catch a flick," Linda said. "Not to waste the *exotic* afternoon downtown."

How many times do you run a scene before the penny drops?

Later, Emil sits in his Parkdale apartment looking at the beech leaf that's now a crinkled chip, strangely pliable.

Linn is setting the table for their Beijing feast. In his armchair, Seriously, green and yellow stuffed, has an eye on the clock, paws in the air.

Emil delves into a stack of designs.

He recalls the Rileys' tinted window—lowering. Barry says something Emil cannot decipher above the engine. Barry's 'We'll never get out of here' comic look, brushing everything aside. Linda pent up, flushed from breast to ear. Snapshot of the afternoon, and Riley history with Emil.

No wonder Emil stood so long at the corner of Clinton and College. His thumb along the blunt teeth of a leaf.

"I will make a *lavita*," Emil tells Linn. "A Transylvanian peasant bed. Very basic, very sound. Queen-sized."

"For us?"

"Linda and Barry," he says. "You plant its four legs in the ground. It needs a bench beside, so you can step up."

"Reconciliation, is this?"

Emil flips through Romanian assignments he completed, or was still working on, since Buchenwald came along: wooden saddles, hand-propelled weeding tools, restored timber barns, Prince Charles's grand four-posters.

"Chinese puzzle, more like." This most fertile period of his life, haunted by the space on a Weimar hillside.

Carve pretty artifacts all you like Emil Benedetti-Toc, his voices tell him. The Rileys make amends and you are deaf.

"Come here, Linn," he says, leaping up. "Grab this bloody thing." Emil holds out the beech leaf, now the texture of hide—tobacco shade.

"Tug!"

You don't play the holocaust for excuses, Emil. Tape your mouth shut, slam all doors, saw wood. You were hateful to your friends. You went too far. Like your brother did.

Emil and Linn tug—a tug o'war.

"Pretend it's a cracker!" shouts Emil. Linda and Barry deserve pardon for their weaknesses, and an apology for yours. Not a bed. The particulars are clear enough now.

"Twist it," Linn says.

The beech leaf snaps and Emil falls backwards, sending the monkey flying.

"Come eat," Linn says, discarding the scrag. "Here's a moldy bedspread for your *lavita*."

It lands amidst the lollipop furniture on Emil's mantel.

"Crèche rug and a counterpane," Emil declares, slinging his own bit of leaf onto the shelf. "A *lepedeu* with toothy trim, to sleep under."

Linn looks doubtful.

"I'll finish the bed by Three Kings Day," Emil says enthusiastically, rescuing Seriously from beneath a chair. "Deliver it to the Rileys personally by rent-a-van."

"Queens take longer, I suppose?" Linn replies, tapping spoonfuls of rice into his bowl.

"If you can see to think."

PINK VIRGIN OF KFC

Not quite thrown. Guan Dai-tai was nudged unceremoniously through the Beijing station gateway into its busy hall. Her parents and Aunt Xiang tut-tutted, vigilant at her heels.

Mandate of heaven, Dai-tai thought, as she stared defiantly at the amber light of a timetable with its crescent window above. Dai-tai stood in her flimsy summer dress and sandals, the black strapped ones that felt like Kit's fingers around her ankle, as her mother strained to see an arrival time for the Shanghai train.

"Platform four," said her mother. "Waiting Hall Number One?" Her husband and sister could not read.

They sailed up the escalator.

Dai-tai crossed her arms. Life was over. In a few minutes, she would greet a stranger—"Golden Husband," as Aunty Xiang put it. She, after all, tracked the betrothable down, without internet or much literacy, through a byzantine network of distant relatives littered between her Sichuan village and the boulevards of Shanghai.

All Dai-tai could think of was Kentucky Fried Chicken.

Colonel Sanders haunted her—woven into recollections of Kit from the United States, their winter mornings and Kit's breath upon her shoulder. Spring Festival jiving when, so close to him, she felt his chest hum. Gunpowder, firecrackers, and a lakeside night when stinging eyes concealed the joy she felt.

In spite of their age difference (Kit was twenty-five, thinning-haired and bespectacled. Colonel Sanders was a permanent, puffy, middle-age), the men merged in Dai-tai's mind. Brand and boy. She could not tell them apart anymore. One on a box of chicken. The other, ground beneath her feet. Ground she must step from, tidbit by tidbit.

How could Kit have behaved like this? Flung her like a chicken in a slaughterhouse.

On entering the station, Dai-tai had noticed the Colonel's tell-tale, white goatee and glasses: origin and solace of her downfall. His mugshot lurked beneath a stone portico, at this art-deco building's western end, slapped on the wall like Chairman Mao's visage in Tiananmen Square.

What was it about American faces?

Bu yao lian. Shameless face. 不要脸。

She felt like vomiting.

Dai-tai in Beijing train station—in KFC land—squirming, paraded. She would marry Chinese, the happy-go-lucky, no-name bachelor of fifty years who played mahjong in teahouses, like many men from Chengdu, his Sichuan hometown—and hers. For the last decade, "Golden Husband" resided in Shanghai and was an amateur actor. He worked in the biggest jade store off Nanjing Road and would one day become sales manager.

In snakehead Aunty Xiang's estimation, "Golden Husband" was a respectable catch. After Dai-tai's 'foreigner incident' it had taken the length of a Summer Olympics to arrange this match.

Dai-tai was eighteen years old. With your beak snapped off, what could you say?

In her time with Kit from Brooklyn, New York—when *they* ran out of things to say, which was surprisingly often—Dai-tai would gaze at the left of Colonel Sanders' face. At America. His face in shadow, so hard to make out, its sootiness blue, down the chicken king's forehead, temple, cheek and chin.

An art of outlines, she supposed. Darkness creased from the nose to nook of an old mouth. Those 1950s specs, a suggestion of bushy eyebrow, silken point of beard. Everything dribbled and defined in black. Beneath the string bow tie doing its splits.

Today, in her glance at KFC, Dai-tai saw closer.

A look of absence. Ashen eyes, into which you tumbled—to buy chicken and, for an eat-in moment, live the cowboy USA, and *be happy like them*. Fresh, hot, and juicy.

Lips torn out, a paper-cut. Had they altered the Colonel's lighting? Or had she never inspected him this way? As though he were a lantern. Between those raven fissures and their white-cheek peaks was *colour*: a sepia gouache—or rouge—as though Sanders spilled some blush. A dab of 'peril' that fluffed the collar of his shirt—a wing, anyway—and stained his apron.

Buckaroo bone a-glowin'? In the August heat.

Dai-tai despaired of this residual, life-without-Kit. She missed wrenching caps from Gatorades, Kit's terror of dogs that barked. His scalding kiss that gobbled up her lips. The tongue writhing in. Was this really love? Red buckets, red walls, the *chewing*? Could you miss all that?

Dai-tai had introduced him to every Beijing KFC. So many, she lost count. For three months, they toured the eateries. It was all Dai-tai could think of, besides places with "Heaven" in their name: temples, parks, a happening bar or two.

After that first night in Tuanjiehu Road. When the scruffy young Westerner slipped in through the Colonel's doors, past a co-worker's feverish mopping. 11:00 p.m., closing time.

Dai-tai pouted. She tried to raise her tiny breasts, nestled beneath the pink KFC t-shirt. "Anne" askew at the pocket, turning this way and that. Look at me, look at me. She stared at him until her face felt hot. She smoothed her hands on green army-pants. A girl alongside took his order while Dai-tai fumbled over a wallop of nuggets.

The Yankee was no doubt a "Mandarin moron" as her KFC friends termed it. Clueless foreigner with "*Xiexie*" and "*Zaijian*" as sole vocabulary—thank you, goodbye—pointing at menu pictures in between.

Cute, very cute.

Was this one cute?

Then you marvelled at Westerners' audacity as well as their sexy-stupid mistakes. Their physical *ugliness*. Especially the overweight Europeans and Russians, the bald and gawky brigade. Huge, round-eyed and bellied, strawberry noses. Why did the malformed come to Beijing? Were *they* grain-fed and hormone free? Aliens, so bilious and bleached. Whatever happened to Western attractiveness? To the Brad Pitts and David Beckhams? In Hong Kong, were they? Clooney, Gere, royal Harry and William? Lurking in Shanghai? Taipei?

No head-turners ever reached the capital.

Let alone KFC, Tuanjiehu Lu.

Something, though, had ignited between Dai-tai and U.S. standard brickface. She held her breath. As the *lao wai* queued for his chicken bucket.

"*Ni fei chang xing gan*," he said to her suddenly, in perfect Chinese. You are very sexy. "你非常性感"

Dai-tai's world folded into the wrap and fries before her.

"*Bu keqi*," she replied. Not at all.

This was no "Mandarin moron."

Showing off her English, Dai-tai said, "You are from America?"

"*Jiu xiang ping guo pai yi yang ju you mei guo te se*," he answered, drumming his fingers on the tray. "Brooklyn, New York."

Dai-tai smirked at the heavily accented Mandarin. 'American as apple pie,' she thought he said. Whatever that meant. 就像苹果派一样具有美国特色.

America's order arrived.

Dai-tai smiled again. Dry city at unexpected typhoon.

From her perch at the counter, before a phalanx of customers, she glimpsed Mandarin-speaking *him* eating alone at a booth. A stranger shifted tables to join him. It was a crowded night. Then another local and another. He looked bothered by the crush. They were Chinese. He was not.

She wrote her cellphone number on a special-offer leaflet, 'We Do Chicken Right'—and headed for the washroom.

On her way, Dai-tai collected several trays. She caught Brooklyn, New York's eye and grinned, indicating the note between forefinger and thumb. He beamed as if someone had sprayed "Have Me" on her face. She went to his table and stacked three cartons. Dai-tai prayed that her colleagues had not noticed the petal falling to his wrist; that the foreigner would be cool. Such a brazen act could cost the job. She was still at high school, needed *kuai* for university in September.

Back at her post, everything seemed finger lickin'.

At midnight, he was waiting at China Post.

"*Wo neng song ni hui jia me?*" he said excitedly, again in thickly accented Mandarin, as though showering himself, as well as her, in ticker tape. "Can I walk you home?"

"我能送你回家么?"

She ducked and led the way.

They walked north along Tuanjiehu Lu, past the bank and travel agency to the main road—"*Gongti*"—where she stopped him, opposite Chaoyang Kosaido Golf Club.

It was January. An icy wind slipped between the high-rises.

"Show me the Jing?" he suggested, this time in English, obviously rating her hip-ness. "Sanlitun? Suzie Wong?"

Dai-tai giggled, pulled her scarf more tightly around her sore, winter throat. "Tomorrow night for sure."

He hesitated.

"You have my number," she said.

"Yes, yes." He pouted in a way that made her smile.

She crossed the busy lanes unescorted.

"*Ni fei chang xing gan!*" he choked out, a second time, tones every which way in the cold. You are very sexy.

41

She had had her fill, linguistic and otherwise, for the night. Did he know any other phrases? She should have left cuteness at that. And split for good.

Of course she did not.

Like most foreigners, Kit was an open book.

Or easy re-invention.

It hardly mattered. Funny and glamorous, he was a find. Even though Dai-tai's schoolmates ridiculed her naiveté. Western boys were notoriously unreliable. The worst cheats. Which was why, unlike Chinese men, they bought so many presents and rehearsed those habitual phrases. *You are very sexy. Can I walk you home?*

Did Guan Dai-tai know nothing?

In the "Jingle Jungle," Kit cobbled together an existence for himself... a three-month 'fast-track' Mandarin course at Peking University (a Harvard Program) along with "Asian Business Practice." Down time all-nighters messaging buddies back home. A pair of "Language Exchange" students for English conversation (pocket money, lust). Thrice-weekly, rather fevered workouts at the gym.

He was lonely as hell.

That was Dai-tai's take.

Like a running dog, Kit wanted in.

"What does it mean?"

On their final day (unbeknownst to her), nestled in Dai-tai's warm, fragile arms, Kit was listening to a pedlar cycling by—"*Tan mian hua!*"—the baritone echoed in the rear courtyard of the Guan family's low-rise building. 'Burning questions' was Kit's second name.

"'Flick the feathers,'" she told him, unsure. "He stuffs duvet covers."

"He *brings* the feathers?"

"Of course."

"I see."

"He's covered in them."

These March, bedroom mornings, highlight of Dai-tai's adolescence, burned into her heart. Parents at work, for an entire month she skipped school, and her prized art-classes. She invited Kit home.

The neighborhood cameras and block leader caught it all.

Dai-tai would never have allowed Kit to steal her innocence. But in January, soon after they met, he confided that his parents died three years before—in a car accident on Cape Cod. Without siblings and in possession of a hefty inheritance, Mr. America was suddenly not just a dangerous, if titillating, diversion. He was a prospect.

In China—well, at Number Eight Middle School, Tuanjiehu KFC and in the tales of Pu Songling—you dreamt of whoppers like this. No head of the man's family to deal with. No inconvenient brothers. Kit would always be hers. Alone. Eat your fingers off, class of 2008!

In jumped Dai-tai. So did Kit, she thought.

"What does *that* say?" Another question.

"'*Shou po lan er lou!*'" she sang, caressing Kit's forearm to the rhythm, growing a little impatient. "'Recycling.'"

"Hard to believe we're in downtown Beijing."

"'*Mo jian zi qiang cai dao,*'" she sang. "Don't ask me what it means, either. Come on! Get up!"

Kit struggled into jeans and coat. "Well?"

"'Sharpen the scissors, sharpen the knives,' dummy," she said, cheeks ablaze. "You really don't know Mandarin, do you?"

"It's like 'A Chorus Line' out there," Kit replied, looking out at the willow tree, and bare branches against a wall. "That duvet guy's got an opera singer's voice."

"Lullabies for housewives," quipped Dai-tai. She climbed into her school uniform. "Hurry, chop chop."

"Why are the kids laughing?"

"They tease the feathers man," she said, "because he can't keep his bike steady."

Kit seemed puzzled. Whitewashed, Dai-tai liked to call it. He often looked like that. "How do you say 'Capital airport' honey?"

Except on this particular morning, Kit's expression was one any block leader would have recognized.

'Thank you' and 'Goodbye.'

DUCKS OF BERLIN

The tour was almost over. She could hang on for another half hour.

Late afternoon in a wet, uncommonly brisk November. As was the custom at Brandenburg Gate, Christiane Bucur led the tourists from the 'Berlin Highlights' bus. A leg-stretching break from scripted observations about the German capital.

She pointed in the direction of the obvious…and informed the Australian trio, and solitary Brit in plastic mac, that if they were tardy, their penalty was to offer a spectacle. Two minutes late, a dance. Five minutes, a song and dance.

Over-exercised humour, her face gaunt.

"How long do we have, then?" said one of the Australians.

"Hurry, the light's fading," she told him.

Today, the sky really was unusually sombre.

Confronted thus by a 'Romany' alien, slyest of the sly, the camera-wielders rushed to their Gate. Christiane's tone placated any sightseer. No-one ever missed the resumption of a Bucur journey. Unspoken time-limits did the trick.

Come hell or high water, she told herself, gazing across Eberstrasse at lamps lit, headlights on. Thursdays before dark, we circle the *Tiergarten*.

A hefty shadow pursued Christiane Bucur.

In two years since the attack, she had been unable to shake it off. At her ear, poking an elbow—the black ape she started to name it—crept and crawled. She knew it was the memory of her assassin Adrian Benedetti-Toc. Brother of her childhood love, Emil. Incision to the neck. Nothing could lessen the terror of an enraged figure striding along a corridor.

Last evening in the Kreuzberg apartment, she made no mention of her nightmares and their daytime skeleton. The celebration with husband Norbert, daughters Magdalena and Gisela, and Emil who was in Berlin for mere days, was about her recovery from attempted murder and its aftermath.

That very morning, Dr. Lehmann of the Mitte Clinic declared her well. In time, the insomnia would clear, he said. Unpleasant dreams were inevitable, but would dissipate.

It had been an arduous twenty-four months. Christiane changed careers. The return to her government office, any office, was more than she could stomach. At thirty-three, she became a novice tour guide.

Chased by the ghost of an infuriated, jilted man with Opinel knife at the ready.

"Drink, Emil," said Norbert joyfully, opening more of his hometown Weimar brew. "My wife's a changed woman."

Emil raised his glass.

Christiane offered cheese and rye bread. There was Linzer torte to follow, and Turkish coffee from the restaurant downstairs.

The two girls, proud of their mother, wore taffeta.

Emil harped on his familiar note. "Maybe I want to stay in Berlin."

"Never content," Christiane said.

Emil was worse than her shadowy stalker. She recalled far happier days in Viscri, Romania, where they would piggyback from school. Taking turns. How she fretted about him.

"Will you ever find a home, Tick Toc?"

"Not for all the tea in China."

Emil was again heading back to Canada from Transylvania. A short leave on this occasion, wherein Emil scouted woodworking contracts.

Most of his sadness, he had her believe, arose from his relationship to the Ontario lakeshore factory—in particular to Mr. 'Taffy' Diewick. A bellied Welshman of poor hygiene, in his misfiring fifties, who saw little opportunity in Emil. Regardless of Emil's fine carpentry skills, and the rare, private contract he, so the boss said, was a disappointment. "You always seem somewhere else, Emil."

Tonight she lost all patience with her old friend's whining. What did he expect of paid employment? Of an outfit making letter-sorting shelves? Of Canada? His city?

To many, his life was thriving.

"So you still carve mailroom "furniture" instead of art," she said dryly. "It's not full-time and you're well compensated. What's the matter with you?"

"I'm wasting myself."

Christiane chuckled.

"In Romania, people would kill for your talents and a big salary in Canada," she said. "Look how often you come back to Europe. Do you see Norbert and I coming west? We can't afford such things. He's a printer."

Emil looked away.

Christiane knew why.

His arrogant opinion unchanged, and irritating, that immigration was too tough a burden, trying to accommodate the adopted country—rather than it you. Toronto, his friends the Rileys, Diewick's, his lover Linn. Failing him.

Everyone but Emil made strides.

"You have your city, your home," she told him. "Look at it as hard as I look at mine, and live."

Christiane is remembering Emil as the "Berlin Highlights" driver Henning re-boards their chocolate and cream double-decker bus. She steps out of the rain and follows him.

"Too dark today," he says, evidently impatient about the final *Tiergarten* shift. "Too dark for you, Christiane."

Henning is a grizzled, highly strung, forty-year-old Bulgarian Jew. Small, soft grey eyes that speak of endurance. He has seen too much of Germany's metropolis, immigrants, dumb tourists. Henning exists for his cherished Vietnamese girlfriend, Tuyen—"whose name means ray," he likes to mention. "The rest of Berlin sucks."

"Four punters in a storm," he curses, scratching his head, "What about your health, Christiane?"

The passengers clamber to the upper deck—each soggy visitor breathless, no-one especially rested on the Bucur tour—wondering, of course, about the time.

"Move those freaks to the teddy-bear bus, why don't you?" Henning says, indicating a yellow double-decker further along Brandenburg Gate. "Let's shut up shop. 'Rain Stopped Play.'"

"It's not far now, Henning."

He dons a brown peaked cap, and slams the window shut.

Christiane sighs, her lip trembles. "Such light you carry."

Henning revs the engine and moves into early evening traffic. Rain thunders down.

Reaching for her jumbo-size manual, notes and microphone, Christiane begins the commentary.

"We now head north-west to the *Reichstag*," she announces, seating herself on the lower deck where there was no-one. "Germany's parliament, the *Bundestag*. Built in the 1880s, it boasts the magnificent glass dome designed by Sir Norman Foster in 1995 which fills the subdued Wilhelmina structure with daylight....Beyond it, the river Spree in one of our classic Berlin downpours... No surprise, is it...that our city's name comes from the Slavic word 'swamp'...?"

Henning, however, has different notions about "our" city—and Christiane Bucur. A "Jewish Tour" instead, the shorter of their company's itineraries.

"Better yet, no tour at all." He steers his bus the opposite way. "What do foreigners know?"

Head buried in her notes, Christiane is trotting out how people send their teddies—Paddingtons, Gund Snuffles, Winnie-the-Poohs, every manner of bear—on organized, sometimes world tours.

"You will probably see one of the yellow double-deckers on our excursion today."

She is oblivious to the magnitude of Henning's turn. It is wet, gloomy, the road congested. Of course their brown double-decker veers this way and that. She takes no notice, trying to get the stuffed-animals' information right.

Like the recent four-horse charioteer atop the Gate, Henning charges east on Unter den Linden.

"'Travelling Teddy Limited'" attendants behave like any other guides," Christiane goes on. "The excursions are sold out every year."

Turning the microphone off, she once more consults her jumbo script. Microphone on and she begins delivering several passages from the Reichstag Fire Decree of 1933 whereby Chancellor Hitler turned an arson attack to his advantage, "Much like conspiracy theorists say of America's leadership and September 11th."

Not once does Christiane glance at the spattered windows. After daylight falters, she rarely looks. Henning knows the routes blindfolded, and her timing of each detailed paragraph.

Off goes the microphone. She rehearses another segment.

On.

Outside the window, there is no *Reichstag* at the Berlin State Library or, "to our left" Humboldt University, and "at right" the Berlin State Opera's version of the Chinese classic 'Journey to the West.'

"The Aqua Dome is next."

Henning has crossed the river twice. No Aqua Dome.

"They take photos of their bears enjoying the sights," she says of the Teddy attendants on the yellow buses, returning to a point she forgot. "Hopping on and off. Every bear is sent home with a holiday scrapbook and DVD."

Off.

Personally, she thinks the teddy-people are lunatics. She finds it hard not to laugh. And, instead, her thoughts turn again to Emil. These past two years, Christiane repeatedly advised him to curtail, even end his own runabouts—"fruit loops" she called them—between Toronto, Romania and Germany. At best he could not afford so many tickets, at worst he alienated his Canadian partner. Emil had paid no heed, and now Linn was lost, and not that long ago.

She is perturbed by Emil's listless voyages of grief, curiosity, inspiration—in part because, at times, she craves them herself. All Romanians do. But also because, for all his peregrinations, he finds no home. Christiane's schoolfriend arrives nowhere—often harming or losing altogether the love of those who were once close.

She bristles at these strains upon her.

Turning on the microphone, Christiane launches into aspects of a vast *Tiergarten* park, "…once the hunting ground of high nobility. This is Berlin's green heart and soul surrounded, at its fringes, by diplomatic missions. Today's trip wends its way around this wooded oasis in the centre of the city, in summer a place of picnics, walks and grilling…."

Henning, meanwhile, is well past a major baroque cathedral and the Palace of the Republic—in rush hour, dual-carriageway traffic—en route to Alexanderplatz and the 'Barn District.' Few trees or fancy gardens to bother anyone there. He will be in Tuyen's arms by eight o'clock.

"Some people get to see cities by bear," Christiane tells everyone, between rehearsing the next lines, clutching her microphone. "Not everyone can travel abroad. My daughters are sending their Gund Snuffles to Cape Town at Christmas."

Night has fallen.

Someone is ringing the bell.

Did she have the mike on? Christiane clicks it back and forth, blows into the mouthpiece, resumes her narration.

Ting-a-ling. Ting-a-ling.

She feels scared.

Henning is grinning like a Cheshire cat. He yowls something dire to the cabin roof, pounds his fist at it several times.

Christiane buries her face in her hands.

"We're at the Victory Column, aren't we?" She sorts through the papers. "I haven't been looking."

Sifting, static.

Is there something wrong? Not certain she hears the audio system clearly. Whose whistling is that?

Sound of footsteps along a corridor.

The leafing on her lap.

Is the microphone on?

Squeaky soles upon a polished floor? She recalls the *Rotesrathaus* government office. Adrian coming up behind her.

Searing pain below her jaw.

She peers through the glass, rubs the condensation from Adrian Benedetti-Toc, at tail-lights and trucks. Not a Column in sight. Christiane shudders. Head to head with a cold, cruel man.

Ting-a-ling. Ting-a-ling. Someone is ringing the bell.

"I've lost my place," she mutters.

She can't look away from the face. So reminiscent of Emil.

"Stop following me, Adrian." Her eyes gleaming in the window. "Please."

Ting-a-ling. Ting-a-ling.

Christiane takes up a section of her manual and blurts into the mike. "Viktoria, the goddess of Victory...."

One of the Australians has come down.

"Hey, love!" a voice chirps. "Aren't we going a bit skew whiff?"

She lays a reassuring hand upon the Gore-Tex shoulder.

"Ain't no "wooded oasis" out of our windows, babe," he says, indicating the railway station alongside. "Whose city are you playing at?"

Christiane nods apologetically, tears streaming across her cheek.

She gestures to possibilities on the other side of the street. Unbelievably, an Alexanderplatz subway sign greets her.

"*The U-bahn!*" she says, turning to the driver as he lumbers the bus along Karl Liebnechtstrasse. "How could you do this?"

Christiane hammers on Henning's cabin window.

"Getting you home, *fräulein!*" His dove-grey eyes.

"Is this about your girlfriend?"

Henning winks.

"Blimey, fellas," the Australian says, joined by his compatriots. "It's 'Bat Out of Hell' down here."

Christiane tosses him the microphone.

"Round and round like ducks," she tells the Australian, as Henning guns his chariot through Alexanderplatz. "You can't go wrong."

A BEIJING MINUTE

Sun Mee turned away from her husband. Nothing, not even ripe long-distance travellers, could counter the stench of Yuanjin's feet.

Or rather, foot.

The left. Socked and shoed as it inevitably was (Yuanjin would never be seen in sandals) on this hot August in Beijing. A cotton-mouth spell that turned all nature rank. As shining trains hastened away, like eels, to Moscow, Pyongyang, Ulan Bator.

The Shanghai express, with precious cargo, was late.

Sun Mee and Yuanjin were unfamiliar with Dongbianmen station. In their early thirties, here to meet their adopted son, they shuffled along with the crowd through an entrance into the vast lobby. The opening bars of 'Happy Birthday' echoed in the noisy vault of a place; trailed by announcement after announcement, '*Qingdao…*' it would begin—'please go to…'—before the words evaporated into hullabaloo as passengers made their way. Yuanjin pointed to an escalator.

"Waiting Hall Number One is for Shanghai," he called to his wife, indicating the upper level.

"I don't think that's right," Sun Mee replied. But could see no alternative.

The couple rose to the second floor. He, a financier for Junan Guoti Securities (Beijing). She, an English tutor from Sichuan Province. 'Happy Birthday' ping-ponged out again.

Odd that the nippy foot-odour stalked Sun Mee today, when their only child, Yuan, was about to arrive. At the apartment in Hong Kong, later in

Beijing, for seven childless years she had endured Yuanjin's left-foot noisomeness. Now, the odour itself was prompting her, 'no.' No, to Yuanjin's project. Today you must make the decision, it said. This really is your final chance. You have been a coward.

Anything to do with children, as in young pregnancy or the birth of dear, sweet girls, was victual for the urge to scram. Spring Festivals, this year's Siberian winter, the earthquake, no event under the sun would soften the heart of her village's Party secretary. Sun Mee could never go home. In Sichuan, she had gambled with maternity. And lost. In Beijing, Yuanjin's widower-father called her 'used goods.' When he was alive, the ancient man would say it within her earshot. Now that he was eighteen months dead, his reproof sounded all the louder. No matter how much Yuanjin had, at one time, consoled her.

Sun Mee wanted to run. So rash a move. So grave a betrayal—of Yuanjin and now Yuan—that, until two months ago, with the discovery of a stranger's letters, she had been afraid to act.

Today, though, she was desperate.

In a few minutes, eight-year old Yuan, escorted by his orphanage supervisor Mr. Chen, would be here. With the boy, she had once imagined, came her liberty. How long it had taken to secure the moment. Eighteen months of correspondence, interviews, trips to a Shanghai Child Welfare Institute. Twenty-five thousand U.S. dollars for the rarity of a male; deformity free, full hearing, 20/20 vision, no insanity. Other buyers would simply flout the law and use a trafficker.

Yuanjin, aloof and meticulous, had signed Yuan up for the Beanstalk International School (start date, September 1st), hired a perky live-in ayi to "aunty" him (already installed). Enlisted their son in junior golf coaching (day after tomorrow). Yuan would walk into "paradise," Yuanjin and his father called it.

Sun Mee had prepared the bedroom. Orchids. Thomas the Tank Engine 'Full Steam Ahead' wallpaper that rollicked toward curtains. For several weeks, Sun Mee painted ornate trim, and the ceiling. She did her best and grumbled that Yuanjin did not hire a decorator.

The adoption was Yuanjin's mission. As though *birth* would right all wrong. The fussy zeal irritated her and emphasized the separateness of their lives. A gap that, two years before, had grown deeper following the demise of Yuanjin's father, and the move from Hong Kong to Beijing.

At first, Sun Mee thought she could love the child Yuan. Four times, she and her husband visited him—accompanied the boy to a park near the Shanghai institute. Good-natured, the youngster dutifully played on a climbing frame. Swung on the silver swing. Uncertain, at first, that she and Yuanjin would watch. Observe they did, and Sun Mee's stomach clenched. Yuan was a dimple-cheeked, shy, intelligent lad.

Who could not love him?

Sun Mee could not.

She was unready, her life hardly begun. This was New China, an Olympics country. Who needed Yuanjin or a family? A *past*? The more her husband groomed Yuan's prospects, the more she craved a future of her own. She had saved money. She could launch a t-shirt business in Houhai, start a language school in Sanlitun. Yuanjin had no time for Sun Mee's ideas or her opinions on adoption. To him, Yuan's destiny was obvious—a maintaining of his own family's ambitions. Mother, home. Only once did her husband waver in his resolve. A year ago, twelve months after his father's death, and Yuanjin still grief-stricken; and six months into the adoption procedures, he had said, "Could you be a sound mother?"

"What do you mean?"

"After your village 'Weeping Room'."

Yuanjin was referring to Sun Mee's twin babies, girls, 'taken away.' Newly settled in Beijing, Sun Mee did not have the conviction to say anything more than, "Of course."

"In spite of my father's view of you?"

"*Because* of it," she had replied, feigning defiance.

Why had she not spoken up? Or reflected upon Yuanjin's brand of grief for a father he purportedly never loved, or forgave for sending him to college in England instead of America? Would Yuanjin make a good father? It was a question that preyed on *her*. Yuanjin might be all Yuan would have.

She drifted through the adoption march, and plotted freedom. Sun Mee was unaware, until very recently, that her husband had weighed options of his own.

Absolution for Yuanjin, however, the private person who grew cold in marriage, would require more than an adopted boy. She could not pardon her husband's seven year about-face. Where was the teasing, fond Yuanjin? That carefree, raucous joker who playfully slapped his thigh, and hers? Now niff-footed, cheating, ramrod. A ghost of a husband, really—a sometime brute with a temper—who no longer made love.

At the far end of Waiting Hall Number One hung a massive painting, *Locomotive in Scottish Mountain Valley*. The train was barrelling through tunnels, over viaducts, around a bend and into the afternoon. Sun Mee's best friend Hongmei, one of her students, had briefed her about the Qing dynasty railway building. Sun Mee gazed at the fifty-foot high ceiling and mud-coloured, art-deco chandeliers.

Why Scotland?

The highland terrain contrasted sharply with the jam-packed throng in the room. Wind-blown, russet complexions, tired clothes that spoke of far-off hamlets, towns, and villages like her own, of Inner Mongolia, and Tibet. Places that jolly steam engine would never find. Surely the hall did more than accommodate people awaiting a Shanghai train? Had Hongmei erred in directing them inside the building? There were hundreds of travellers in this upper-level Waiting Hall. Did you *wait* from here or *depart*?

Sun Mee stewed.

Had others noticed the state of Yuanjin's foot—shifting with its odourless other on the grey and brown tile? Like puff-puffing smoke in the distant artwork, Yuanjin's foot-reek billowed into the cavernous hinterland. She recalled attempts, before their marriage, to subdue it with baking soda and ground yellow Daikon radish. Vodka baths, and regular appointments at the 'foot massagist's soup wash' in Golden Dragon Hutong. The remedies were no remedy. Too late now. Take your leave of him, the stench cried out.

Yuanjin's slow footsteps.

Rebuke?

A dare?

Opposite a chili-chicken vendor, Sun Mee and her husband found a row of seats. 'Happy Birthday' boomeranged from the tartan train, 'Qingdao…' —'please go to…'

The couple sat down. Two pairs of feet between steel legs.

"Go *on*," Sun Mee said to herself.

It's time, the foot-pong pinged.

Two months before, as Sun Mee daubed paint on drawers and cupboards in the sleeping quarters for Yuan, she discovered a packsack belonging to her husband. He must have overlooked it. Yuanjin was scrupulous about possessions. She undid the bag. It held finance texts from his graduate school in Durham, England. Letts pencil case, Sony calculator, and rental receipts for a property on Magdalene Street 'near Bankside Post Office' (scrawled in red and underlined). Large manila envelope.

Wrapped in a Burberry scarf was a cache of twenty or so notelets from someone called Leo. Evidently from Durham, and not a student.

Sun Mee paused.

Yuanjin kept papers and diaries in a locked filing cabinet in his study.

Sun Mee's English was impeccable. Why not read a few pages?

Leo sounded affectionate, perhaps flirtatious. He owned a plastics company, Durham Upshaw's, and was much older than a twenty-three-year-old Yuanjin. He signed his messages, 'With love and cuddles, your bishop boy.' There were nude photographs of Yuanjin and Leo. Three close-up shots of her husband in a bejewelled thong. Another of Yuanjin posing on a staircase landing. The two men in a rowboat, 'Windermere Hunks' in pencil on the reverse—with a sentence, in Mandarin, about *Four Gentlemen*.

Sun Mee touched her forehead.

What blazed from the correspondence, and the fact that her husband stored it, was passion. Judging from later word, however, which Yuanjin also filed chronologically, Yuanjin left England, without Leo, for Hong Kong where Yuanjin's father had found his son employment with Junan Guoti Securities' head office.

Seated on parquet flooring, Sun Mee turned the page:

'I hope you find the kind of love I felt for you and still do feel. Get over it, you will say again. I have tried very hard. It is obvious I loved you more deeply than anyone ever....'

The 'agony column' from Leo in County Durham to Yuanjin in Hong Kong went on for months:

'While I can guess your reasons for the cold shoulder, I want you to know that what I'm offering is not anger or retaliation or demands. You and I had a great relationship. You said it yourself. There's not a day goes by I do not think of you. It will help bring an end to our connection and set the basis for friendship if you would let go this silence. I don't deserve it and neither do you....'

She felt the anguish of this man. Although these kinds of affiliations were foreign to Sun Mee, what preoccupied her was Yuanjin's conduct. Dropping the man as though he were *delete* upon a screen was one thing. Ignoring him for good? Westerners could be pathetic in love. But Leo was right, no-one deserved such treatment.

There were recent notes, from last year, forwarded from Hong Kong and, again, filed. Leo was indeed persistent—on a mission of his own. Sun Mee smirked at the unknowing impertinence of a lovelorn English 'comrade' unaware of Yuanjin's posting to Beijing two years ago. Her husband was married now, and thirty-three. Yuanjin could have at least informed Leo of the wedding, if not his whereabouts.

But there was a final letter from Leo—Beijing Upshaw's—that Sun Mee read twice:

'Dear Prince of China…I am in Beijing. Your hometown. I have opened a small plant here, and in Shenzhen. I wish you all the best in Hong Kong, and hope that you are overcoming the grief about your father. You are in Hong Kong aren't you? Today I walked in Chaoyang Park. A weekend's a weekend right? I thought I saw you striding by, tall and lean, a 'banana' as you call yourself, 'Yellow on the outside, white on the inside.' I used to enjoy that about you, full of contradictions! I will not come to see you in Hong Kong, if that's where you are, but I'm grateful for news that you are married. Given this development, it's not so unusual, I suppose, that you would wish to risk seeing me once more. You're 'safe' now, isn't that how it goes? The fact that you would consider a reunion "sometime soon" is disturbing. As you once said to me, Yuanjin, the world is not waiting for you. Single as I am, I do prefer a more consistent partner than you have been. It's eight years since you dropped out of my life.

Sincerely,
Leo Upshaw

P.S. Next Saturday, I'm visiting the Great Wall at Mutianyu. Do you remember our visit there? Regards to your wife, if she knows who I am. I hope she fares better than I did.
L.U.

Sun Mee gazed at the word 'reunion,' zipped up the packsack, and held it close. This earnest talk. She could barely believe it. Yuanjin's adventurous, student history and its aftermath was not blessed with any secret cubbyhole in his study. Perhaps he had wished her to find these photographs and letters. He had compelled her to paint Yuan's bedroom, after all. A sign of his resignation about Leo, and indifference to her? Regardless, the relationship with Leo was over. Durham man down.

She pictured Leo and her husband wearing nothing but life-jackets. The Englishman, and the husband she once loved, sharing a joke about their 'Hunks' nakedness and 'spring orchids in a boat.' Did Yuanjin slap his friend's thigh? For many days and nights, she recalled Leo's despairing voice from northern England. Sun Mee pondered how Yuanjin had taken his time to write the man. She marvelled at how Leo, in the end, had moved a wall. Did Yuanjin re-read the letters, and reminisce over the pictures? The foreigner's button penis? Filing the photos neatly. Were the messages sewn into Yuanjin's tight-lipped ways?

One rainy evening, alone in the Tuanjiehu apartment, Sun Mee imagined trudging through an English valley, clambering over a stile, past grazing sheep. She encountered Leo and told him about her Sichuan village, and how Yuanjin had charmed her at the Suzie Wong nightclub in Beijing. She imagined confiding to Leo her desire for an independent life, and her dream of Yuanjin and their son Yuan living with Leo. In darkness, Sun Mee watched the silver ceiling—swing—and its passersby. Could her husband Yuanjin smile? Could Yuan? For a long time, Sun Mee watched.

She wept quietly—and decided not to confront Yuanjin right away. She needed time to formulate a plan. But one June evening, Sun Mee did follow him to an area not far from home. Tuanjiehu Zhonglu, a notorious side street. She guessed the purpose of his forays.

But after those letters...

The spot was near Tuanjiehu Park East Gate. Its 'English Corner' was where she and Yuanjin once dated, before he was shipped off to Durham. Often, they had lingered near a pavement calligrapher, and the elegant brushstrokes that disappeared. Like Yuanjin's smile into a kiss. The touch of his fingers.

She hurried past those gates, and along tree-lined Tuanjiehu Lu. People in silhouette. Metallic air. Casually, she walked into Tuanjiehu Zhonglu. On her left, the familiar row of shops. Tobacco store. The pink front, coloured lightbulbs, and candy-striped pole of a hairdressers—'Manhattan Wave'—that catered to men's, largely Westerners,' needs. Sun Mee approached the window.

Yuanjin in his summer suit was negotiating, alongside a hairdryer, with the establishment's heavily made-up young woman. At first, Sun Mee wanted to think he was purchasing his favourite skin-whitening cream, or those stick-on strips that made his eyes look larger.

Sun Mee knew better.

"Let Taiwanese Barbie enjoy his foot," she said to herself, strangely amused that her husband sought a female. See if a whore can put up with his foulness. Whoever wanted marriage to a real '*tongzhi*,' anyway? A thoroughbred poofter. Yuanjin was stinker enough.

She observed her husband ease aside a doorway of garnet beads that beheld an inner parlour, and divan. In the storefront, Yuanjin's 'Manhattan Wave' girl leaned forward to check herself in a brightly lit mirror.

Even from the street, Sun Mee noticed it—and took a sharp breath. High on Barbie's determinedly flawless throat, perched an Adam's Apple…that swallowed at its reflection.

On her way through Tuanjiehu Park, Sun Mee realized that, with Leo or not, her husband would never turn to her for comfort. Yuanjin would forbid her peace of mind. She composed a letter to Leo requesting that, before the end of July, the Englishman meet her and Yuanjin at their apartment. She wished to "hand over the marriage." In keeping with Yuanjin's method, she addressed the letter to Leo at his company in England, copied to the Beijing branch. She assured Leo it was "the best of news" and that it would "change each of our lives for the better."

Three weeks later, Sun Mee received a reply:

Dear Mrs. Zhao:
It's an honour to receive your proposal concerning Yuanjin and Yuan. I prefer to let sleeping dogs lie.
Sincerely,
Leo Auckland Upshaw

"Is this Waiting Hall for Shanghai *arrivals*," Yuanjin enquired of a unkempt man who had appeared, from nowhere, at the blue plastic chairs.

"We don't know, either," said a sullen young girl, seated with family, next to Sun Mee.

"This is the Shanghai Waiting Hall," the man replied. "For people who are going to Shanghai." He pointed to the 'exit' signs, but not before enquiring casually about their reasons for meeting the train. "Go right once you're out of the building," he told them, unsteady on his feet. "The arrivals gate opens onto Dongbianmen plaza."

Sun Mee turned to see if the young girl had understood the man's directions. When Sun Mee looked back, the helpful visitor had disappeared. "How do we thank him?"

"After he asked all those questions about husbands, and me sitting right next to you?" said Yuanjin, his face flushed.

Sun Mee shrugged.

The girl mimed 'swigging from a bottle.' "Is that your husband next to you?"

"We need to be outside," Sun Mee said, admiring the girl's black-strapped sandals. "The drunk told us."

"I'm Dai-tai," she replied. "From Sichuan Province, like I explained to that guy. These are my parents, and Aunty Xiang."

"Sun Mee."

The Sichuan women nodded.

"I hope my 'Golden Husband' doesn't show," Dai-tai began.

"Come on," said Yuanjin, pulling at his wife's arm. "The train must have arrived by now."

Sun Mee stood up.

"Your student Hongmei is to blame," Yuanjin told her. "You should not have relied on such an inexperienced person."

Sun Mee followed him downstairs, past the Kentucky Fried Chicken outlet, and Soft Seat Waiting Hall Number Two, and into the stifling heat. Dai-tai, her parents and Aunt Xiang in tow.

Before the arrivals gate, Yuanjin presses his hand on Sun Mee's shoulder. He stands on tiptoe. She feels like a see-saw. "Do these people look like they're from Shanghai?" he asks, as passengers trickle through the doorway and into the crowd.

Sun Mee shakes him off. She is losing all thought of fleeing. Like her husband, she fixes her eyes on the Dongbianmen gate for a sight of their new son Yuan, and his supervisor Mr. Chen.

Several police vans make their way alongside a blood transfusion trailer parked a hundred yards from Yuanjin and Sun Mee. Emergency sirens jar the air. In an effort to let the vehicles through, people press closer. As the convoy halts, a horde of officers runs into the station. Sun Mee watches the rushing policemen, and steals a glance at Dai-tai nearby. The girl is letting her parents and Aunt Xiang monitor the arrivals gate.

This is the moment to run, Sun Mee thinks.

Too late?

"That's them there!" Yuanjin lurches forward.

"No, no." Sun Mee pulls him back. "The boy's with his *mother*."

Yuanjin tiptoes higher, his head tilting every which way.

"There!" he says, jabbing Sun Mee, and forcing himself sideways. "Let's go."

Yuanjin's wife moves forward. She glimpses Dai-tai, who is sobbing at the approach of her 'Golden Husband.'

Sun Mee's knees dither.

A Westerner prizes himself between the distressed Dai-tai and her family. The perspiring man heads in Sun Mee's direction. "Yuanjin!" the foreigner yells. "Yuanjin! Over here!"

Sun Mee's husband looks around, and stares past his wife, at the new-comer. Yuanjin's face is taut.

Leo is here. Sun Mee is astonished.

Leo reaches Yuanjin, and thrusts his hand toward him. "Congratulations on the adoption," he says, his eyes darting.

Sun Mee reaches forward, and shakes his hand.

"Leo Upshaw." He is a blonde, not recently dyed, fiftiesh man in a maroon shirt patched with sweat. He cannot hold a smile. Clutched at his thigh are distressed orchids.

"You visit Beijing again?" Yuanjin says.

"To see you, yes."

"Our son is coming from Shanghai today," Yuanjin replies, and turns nervously toward the gate.

"Mr. Leo knows."

"How does he?"

"Sun Mee?" Yuanjin repeats his question.

"I'm sorry the friendship ended as it did," Leo says.

Sun Mee feels that the romantic *lao wai* is about to kiss her husband.

"I sent him the details," she says.

Sun Mee wonders what a sleeping dog really is.

Yuanjin closes his eyes, a Beijing minute.

"I think we can make it up," Leo goes on, his voice cracking.

Sun Mee imagines the heavyset Englishman has fought battles with himself. To appear at the station. Today.

"Yuanjin," she informs her husband. "Mr. Chen and Yuan are here."

Flustered, her husband turns to greet them.

As people struggle by, Sun Mee and Leo watch Yuanjin. He bows to greet his son.

"*Qing...*"—please—says Sun Mee. She invites the Englishman to join her husband and welcome Yuan.

Leo demurs.

"Prince of China," she reminds him.

Yuanjin looks over his shoulder, joy fading from his eyes.

Sun Mee pushes off.

"Sun Mee?" her husband says, as the boy Yuan and Mr. Chen look at her expectantly. "Come back!"

Sun Mee hurries toward Jianguomen Qiao footbridge.

I have come back, she tells herself. She runs up the steps as if they were burning—across—and down the other side. A smell of boiling sweetcorn and car-exhaust fills her nostrils. I *have*. I'm sure.

Around a bend.

Into the afternoon.

RED WAISTCOAT

NARRATIVE (dressed in red leather coat): The dog of depression entered me around December 1991, before the Christmas lunch at a downtown restaurant. Over months it sunk its teeth into my flesh, until the following summer when I met D.M. Thomas.

Then it tore from the bone.

I was a dog-man.

Preparing for my meeting with the British novelist, I re-read *The White Hotel* about Lisa Erdman's sexual hysteria, the bayonet-rape, lakeside fantasies:

> *I gave birth to a wooden embryo*
> *its gaping lips were sucking in the snow*
> *as it was whirled away into the storm,*
> *now turning inside-out the blizzard tore*
> *my womb clean out, I saw it spin into*
> *the whiteness have you seen a flying womb.*

Eros and Thanatos; love, death. Lisa with Freud's son Martin—curiously I wanted more. In Thomas' *Memories and Hallucinations* I found the genesis of Lisa's experience at a white hotel.

The dog-man ate.

PERSONAL JOURNAL ENTRY. DECEMBER 19, 1991. An end. John collected us in a blue van, without the family dog, Sandy. Frigid lunch hour. Dreaded it. Corporate bash. Sixteen courses at Sung Li Garden. Vehicle stank of dog, burgers and piss. All of us over-dressed. New coats, rustling. Mary, Janice, Natasha (in Christmas red cashmere) and I in the back. John and Sarah (flirting) in front. Perfume. John unsteady on scotch, horseman down the mountain, unloaded us in a parking lot. Was he doing the office a favour? All of us coated in Sandy's dog-hairs. Oh Christ! Natasha hysterical, cursing and baring her teeth at John (she'd been so friendly to him). She wouldn't enter the restaurant. Dropped her green holly pin. Sarah knelt down to her, brushing away as much dog as possible. John grinning. Sarah rose and touched his back. He hates these do's. Must write it up in the New Year: wolf-beneath-red cashmere? "Dog Hairs," a short story. Leaving for England tomorrow. Two weeks.

LICHFIELD DIOCESAN ASSOCIATION OF MORAL WELFARE. CHILDREN ACTS. CONFIDENTIAL VISITOR'S REPORT PENDING LEGAL ADOPTION. MAY 19, 1955. Baby E. was placed in their care just two weeks ago. He settled at once and has been very good on the whole. He was in his pram outside the caravan. Nicely clothed and all the bedding very clean. The garden plot is also well tended.

NARRATIVE (dressed in red leather coat): In *Memories*, Thomas purchases Kuznetsov's *Babi Yar* and hovers over the genocide chapter. Dina Pronicheva, an eye-witness to the massacre and also a victim, manages to feign being shot. At nightfall she crawls from among the corpses in the ravine. In Thomas' mind, this event coalesced with his neglected manuscript, a wild monologue,

The Woman to Sigmund Freud: "There were extraordinary connections. My anonymous heroine had also made a terrified escape from an unspecified danger. I had based her fantasy on the elements: water, fire, earth and air. The lake had flooded, the hotel burned, mourners had been buried in an avalanche, skiers had fallen through the air to their deaths. All these events were echoed at Babi Yar: the victims had fallen into the ravine…later, the Nazis had burned the dug-up corpses, trying to hide their crime; then, under the Soviets, a dam had burst, flooding the ravine and most of Kiev."

PERSONAL JOURNAL ENTRY. DECEMBER 23, 1991 (aboard British Rail from London to Birmingham): Three days in the smoke. Earls Court. Seedy hotel room, elegant Georgian pillars. Damp. Draughts. Walked and walked after visiting Mrs. Givens at St. Catherine's House. She presented all the adoption documents. My birth-mother's name is Smith. SMITH! Stood in St. Paul's afterwards, stunned. How do I find Smith from 1955? Wind and rain as night fell. Later: weird experience at Euston station. Standing under the departure board. A dog came along. Quite carefree it squatted next to me, dumped, and wandered across the plastic floor, tail wagging. No one seemed much bothered. But I couldn't leave the dog alone. Of all the things to be obsessed with in London. I watched as it trotted away, behind travellers' legs. Why stare at a dog? Get a grip. Board the train. Read the news. After three years in Canada, the traitor E. journeys to his adoptive mother's dinner in Birmingham.

P.S. Before my appointment, I saw the Duchess of York with children entering a Drury Lane theatre near Mrs. Givens' office. Sarah Ferguson, just a mother in an open raincoat with her kids. She hurried, unsmiling, past photographers angling themselves like exposed plumbing.

Baby E. now weighs over 15lbs, though plump, is firm and looks contented and healthy. He was very nicely clothed in soft knitted woollies, all fresh and clean. He is strong and active.

NARRATIVE (dressed in red leather coat): Deeper thematic connections developed for Thomas: "*Freud, like most of the early psychoanalysts, had been Jewish. So were most of their patients. One could interpret the psychoanalytic movement as in part a Jewish response to anti-Semitism. The most 'fashionable' problem dealt with was hysteria; mythologically, hysteria was associated with powers of premonition—the Delphic oracle and Cassandra. Might not some of the hysteria treated by Freud have been caused by apprehensions of the future rather than suppressions of the past?*"

LETTER TO THE WRITER J.S. PORTER: Manitoulin Island. August 17, 1992.

Dear John,

Yes, Sandy's the inspiration for "Dog Hairs," which I wrote in February, after the England trip. All credit to your shedding dog. I'm thrilled *Broadway* published it. Thrilled stupid. Some consolation for the clouds on this lake.

Unbelievably, I fell asleep in the Harbour Castle lobby last Friday waiting for my chat with D.M. Thomas. He was understanding. But we didn't have long before the airport. He said I should carry on writing, stay put in Canada, quit doubting my decision to settle here. You suggested I rewrite "Dog Hairs" and tell the real story. How my dog experiences relate to Mrs. Givens' portfolio of reports, and to Euston station. I can't remember now if D.M. agreed.

You know Rilke's letters well, don't you? He writes about looking at some Cézanne paintings with an artist-friend, Mathilde Vollmoeller… Dogs come into it, don't they? Must see you. Come to this rented "cottage," if you can get away. It's a crate with orange carpets. But there's water.

Dog-devils,
E.

LICHFIELD DIOCESAN ASSOCIATION OF MORAL WELFARE. CHILDREN ACTS. CONFIDENTIAL VISITOR'S REPORT PENDING LEGAL ADOPTION. JULY 22, 1955. Baby E. is now about 17lbs. He was fast asleep in the shade of a big tree and had on only light covering. The guardian *ad litem* has called on mother, and a court date set. Mother is so happy to have baby to provide for.

PERSONAL JOURNAL ENTRY. NOVEMBER 1, 1992: Completed the 'real' story of "Dog Hairs." Will be reading it at Valentino's as part of the 'Lit. Chat' evening. I sleep two hours a night.

NARRATIVE (dressed in red leather coat): In *Memories*, D.M.Thomas convinces himself that, "*The terrors suffered by Freud's patients were metaphors of hallucinations of an event such as Babi Yar. Freud strove compassionately over months to lay bare one person's psyche and erotic personality; the Nazis got thirty thousand people to undress—quite without Freudian prurience—then shot them. The white hotel, life, was made for pleasure and happiness; but there was something in its very fabric which demanded self-destruction. These connections occurred to me, mostly in the space of a minute or two, and left me shaking with*

excitement. I now knew that 'The Woman to Sigmund Freud' was the start of a novel that would end at Babi Yar. Eros and Thanatos. It couldn't be anything but The White Hotel."

LICHFIELD DIOCESAN ASSOCIATION OF MORAL WELFARE. CHILDREN ACTS. CONFIDENTIAL VISITOR'S REPORT PENDING LEGAL ADOPTION. AUGUST 15, 1955. Baby E. now weighs over 18lbs and is a rather fat baby. Beautifully clean and well dressed as usual. Mother obviously takes great pride in him. My visits are no longer necessary.

NOTE FROM THE WRITER J.S. PORTER. DECEMBER 17, 1992: There are other Thomases besides D.M., old fella. Thomas Merton has his dogs too, you know. Listen to the tapes. Mathilde Vollmoeller told Rilke that Paul Cézanne sat and painted like a dog. Called by the dog in his work, beaten by the dog that let him starve. Seeing-eye dog. Soul dog. I have poems for you. Soothing ones. Lunch Thursday? I've got the blue van.

PERSONAL JOURNAL ENTRY. FEBRUARY 2, 1993: Valentino's Restaurant. 'Lit. Chat' evening. Three people showed. Marilyn and Rosalind spoke about friends of the black dog. John was passionate about the talk, and about Marilyn and Rosalind. There is something tormenting me.

POSTCARD TO THE WRITER J.S. PORTER. FEBRUARY 6, 1993: I have become sick from lack of sleeping. Went on a walk by Lake Ontario. The ice moaned.

The doctor advises rest. Proust abed! as you would say. I must get better. I don't really follow what you said about Cézanne painting like a dog.

POSTCARD TO THE NOVELIST D.M. THOMAS. FEBRUARY 20, 1993: I'm pleased that you enjoyed my review of *Flying Into Love*. Did you receive the anthology with my story in it? I enclose "The Duchess, Mrs. Givens and the Dog." When is *Pictures* out in Canada?

NOTE FROM THE WRITER J.S. PORTER. MARCH 1ST, 1993: Kundera talks of social awkwardness, my friend—and how out of it come dog-people fully engaged in the world. Dog heads, human bodies. Rilke described a dog seeing himself in a mirror and thinking: there's another dog. But really Rilke is talking about how Cézanne paints. That's what you're trying to grasp. Animal attentiveness. Kundera, he talks about the dog in us as a natural virtue and goodness. Proof that for some of us life is elsewhere. Turning inward. Where poetry lives. You'll be okay. Even Sandy says so! I have more verses for you.

PERSONAL JOURNAL ENTRY. APRIL 16, 1993: No, doctor, I do not see seven white wolves in a big walnut tree in front of the window at night. No, I don't see big foxy tails, stretched claws and immobile wolves stretched to attention. Do you? You seem to mention them a lot. Maybe I can help? Freud was wrong, you know. Didn't you read the papers?

NOTE FROM THE NOVELIST D.M. THOMAS. MARCH 11, 1993. I prepared for the review of Roth's latest book, *Operation Shylock*, by re-reading his *Ghost Writer*. I was so profoundly affected by what I found that I made a confession of my own, right in the review. You might find it of value, given your plight. You will overcome this malaise. You are strong.

New York Times Book Review, March 7, 1993. *"Writers in their lonely struggle with a quill or word processor, are bound to be aware of how many other selves are being excluded from expression; hence their fascination with doubles. The present reviewer should declare a debt of gratitude. After a year of silence and depression, in which he could not read let alone write, he managed slowly to get through 'The Ghost Writer.' It was helpfully short, clear and elegant; also, it reassured him that other writers too feel the danger of writing, the perilous closeness of fact and fiction, and the proximity of the edge."*

PERSONAL JOURNAL ENTRY. APRIL 30TH 1993: Loose pages entitled 'Final Paragraphs of "Mrs. Givens, The Duchess, and the Dog"':

Leaving Mrs. Givens' envelope on the dresser next to some coins, Tom undressed and climbed into a musty, single bed. He extinguished the light. Rain was thrumming against the window. An old velvet curtain lifted with the draught and brushed against linoleum. Heating pipes swallowed. He fell away exhausted. In darkness, gathering the duchess, Mrs. Givens, and the dog to his heart, he knew there would be song. He could hear lips parting. The duchess hurrying to a stage, Mrs. Givens in sensible shoes offering him maps. The Euston dog riding a London Transport escalator going up. The choir was here. He clutched at his sides.

LETTER FROM JOHN FLOOD, RESEARCHER, NATIONAL ORGANISATION FOR THE COUNSELLING OF ADOPTEES AND THEIR PARENTS, OXFORD, ENGLAND. MARCH 8TH, 1993:

I believe I have located the record repositories that hold the 1955 Electoral Registers for the addresses on your original birth certificate. Searching these repositories will allow me to verify which of the two mothers, with certificates enclosed, is yours. Unfortunately, your account is currently overdrawn to the amount of sixteen pounds, thirty-three pence.

POSTCARD FROM THE NOVELIST D.M. THOMAS. APRIL 16TH, 1993: *Pictures at an Exhibition* is due out in Canada from Scribners in October. It's been received mostly with outrage here!! I'm the incarnate devil!! Best wishes.

PERSONAL JOURNAL ENTRY. MAY 1, 1993: Wild dog-man among the ruins. Wild dog-man, are you scorched and buried, shot and drowned, mud stuffed between your grinning? Which of you remains and watches? Man or dog-man? Does either of you live? Who's the birth in this bedroom alcove, scratching matted hair, panting for meat, beaten bloody on a bed? Who takes this executioner's shot, gun-metal kiss upon the lips? Eye to eye we wait. Between the man and dog-man, here walks the wolf, crumpled lightning in a bedsheet. Mouthing orders with a charred tongue, buttoning up his waistcoat, red. Strolling. One leg, two. Like there is a place to go.

SUDDEN MEMORY OF A ROW OF BEECHES

You are jumpy this winter, Emil—and I am all ears, and contortion. Inside your messenger pouch. As twenty-eight year old Hoichi Hinata—"Harry"—offered you the Berlin teddy-guide job.

He did not hesitate employing a Canadian, even a Romanian one. Threw in a basement apartment as a crash for you and your green and yellow monkey-bear.

"That's so cool," he said, pointing at me.

Like an agent with credentials, you show him my mottled face. These cheeks tufty with subway stubs and Wrigley's foil.

"Goes by the name 'Seriously'," you told him.

In *my* state.

Harry was business and futuristic vision, owner of 'Travelling Teddy GmbH.'

"Grub you provide yourself," he said. At McDonald's later, he confided that in Tokyo he developed *hikikomori*. Retreated to his bedroom for a few years. His parents left boxes of food and clean clothes at the door. It was liberation. Sequestered within four walls. Last summer, he vacated his quarters, came to Germany and established the international tour company for toy animals.

"I'm always expanding, expanding," he said, hurling his skateboard at the December frost.

We thundered under Brandenburg Gate. Emil and I ran alongside.

"I've sold franchises in London, Paris, New York, Shanghai," he boasted. "We get teddy-bears from Fiji."

You pretended to be impressed—you needed the euros.

"We charge a lot for digital images," he said. "The sound and video clips."

"Of their teddies in world adventure?"

Harry nodded. "The price is much less than family travel."

You were bemused and not a little afraid that you in your thirties—and the teddy-senders in their who-knows-what—might be lacking something. Like maturity. Or friends.

Yet he paid handsomely, Mr. Hinata. He slept beneath his office desk in the ground floor unit. Unlike your childhood girlfriend Christiane, he wanted you—and me—here.

You'd been working for Harry for a week, and now you were at the Travelling Teddy office on your last fortnight in Berlin.

"*I* decide who does what!" Taffy Diewick blared, on the phone from his Toronto outfit. "Return to Canada and I'll assign you garden outcomes."

Mr. Diewick was proud of the new initiative: to launch into patio ornaments—the "garden outcomes," geese, gnomes—as well as mail-sorting shelves. Legless duck torsos, hewn from bamboo root and imported from Indonesia, were arriving in container loads at the Long Branch factory where Diewick's thirty workers—Eastern Europeans and a hyperactive dwarf from Freelton—carved teak legs and feet. Gluing, nailing them to the sides of fowl. In Ontario's 'rust belt' breezes, the webbed limbs rotated. Taffy's version of a waddle.

"No more cleaning floors and emptying trash all day?" you asked. The bulk of your recent labour at his company, undivulged to Christiane.

The line fell quiet.

"Less of it," the pillock said. "We need tidy workshops, Emil Benedetti-Toc."

"I'm a craftsman, Mr. Diewick, not the housekeeper. You use my name to advertise your brand."

Taffy swallowed. (I hear everything from my bag). "We'll talk."

"No, we've gabbed enough."

I, Seriously, monkey companion, beat my chest, wrappers flying. Emil decisive at last.

"I've accepted a hire in Berlin, then I'm going home, Mr. Diewick."

"Which is?"

"Viscri."

"Romania?"

"Keep your ducks."

"Large, medium and small!" he said. "Canadian backyards can't get enough. Our people hammer those bird boards on overtime. Get your ass to Long Branch, sunshine. Let's get our ducks away."

"Quack," you replied, dropping the receiver to its cradle. "Quack."

Seriously, I'm crumpled for joy, my face in peaks.

You scurried to the bus near Alexanderplatz, an atypical lightness in your step.

You had plans for me too, didn't you, Emil?

I should have guessed.

A matter of juggling dosages, Dr. Lehmann said at the Mitte Clinic. He stuck to his view that Christiane was largely well. That the imaginings were temporary. That you, if you wished, needed to be in town only two weeks more—while her medicines reclaimed their grip. A long-standing friend would do her good, he added. In the morning she might resume her work as a tour guide.

Near midnight, seven days ago—on a bench at Berlin's Tegel airport—you awaited calls for the Toronto flight. Christiane was restless, still distraught from an earlier, aborted circling of the city on her bus tour.

She requested a foot.

You smirked. The boyhood smirk. From a time when you didn't know what you were.

She was serious—and removed one sock, then the other. Your toes were glad of air. She lowered her head and caressed—in all impishness—the undersides of your feet, the heart of an arch, then its brother.

No-one seemed troubled by the antics.

Save you.

I knew you were remembering that row of beeches in Viscri. The smirk said it. Your mountain village where, one early summer after class, the foot pecking started and you made love for the first time. You lay on your back beneath the haphazard line of trees near Alexandru's tavern.

Afterwards, in dappled light you heard her say, "When you stand, don't crush those kisses." You, all trickster, leapt up, an oaf on hot coal stumbling to keep your soles unharmed, from properly touching earth.

How she laughed, you said.

You have never forgotten that day. Of course you remembered this, of all things—in the Hauptgebäude main concourse at Tegel airport—and understood you would not catch the plane for Toronto and return to Diewick's.

I told you so.

I could see you were distressed, fighting the decision, recognizing it was less impulsive than it seemed. This was not about arches, or Christiane's soft lips. It was turnabout. Resolution. About your unfulfilling life—a return home, for good. A notion pressing you for months?

Like Christiane's memories: of a man who tried to kill her.

Eighteen years in Toronto taught you caution, torpor. Canada's legacy to every immigrant: patronized, heading for something that cannot pan out—love, career, friendship. Pinnacles never reached—or available. Income enough to maintain a pulse and the weekly lottery. This was how it felt, you told me, in the true north strong and free.

Not much different from gazing at leaves, in fact, in the shadow of a mosaic tree in Viscri. Sun-yellow, green, brown—the colours of me.

Cracks of blue, uncertainty.

Not the New World you imagined is it, Emil? Freedom, prosperity. In Canadian culture you will progress. Woodworking skills blossom.

"In Toronto, you will find your feet," your father and brothers said.

They were wrong.

You got to see Canada from an upstairs window. Please do not open it. The outside is not yours.

At seventeen, when you arrived in Toronto, you wrote a terrible poem about the place you found. Canada, your promised land. You described the luscious sight that, in Romania, you had imagined—many faces, loving light, gaze up from a big white table. Huge room. Many guests speak kindly. You used the language of Romanian poets, of Eminescu.

Poorly.

At thirty-five, you wrote more verse, equally bad, about another Canada. The one that let you down.

A poem about your lover Linn who likewise disappointed you. Missed you too often, dashed back to China. But not before giving you a monkey teddy-bear—me— to help you overcome the news of Christiane's stabbing at your brother Adrian's hand.

You wrote lines about prurient friends in Brampton—the Rileys—who, missing you, tried to partner-up men you had found and lost.

Who failed whom, Emil? Who does the forgiving? For years you have been unsure.

"Go back to Canada," Christiane says, on the seat at Tegel. "It's where you belong."

"Don't worry," you reassure her, claiming your foot. "I'm not moving in with you and Norbert. I'll work for the bear bus we passed, find a room, keep near until your demon flees, visit my insane brother Adrian, if they let me."

"I want to get ahead, Emil," she said, "not worry about another Benedetti-Toc."

"You're my friend."

"Adrian was a friend also."

"I'm nothing like him," you say. "Besides, he did get you a job."

"Before he tried to kill me."

You remained.

"There is Seriously to decide about too," you tell her.

"Please leave Berlin," she says. "You alarm me as much as your brother. I can't help it."

Hitler's last day is every teddy's darling.

Skirting the site of Berlin's Reich Chancellery, you walk the bears behind an apartment block and sit them on scrubby ground.

Like trees in rows.

"Under us is the *führerbunker*," you say. "Eight metres down."

"Beneath your feet, on April 29th 1945, Adolf Hitler married thirty-three year old Eva Braun, his mistress. The day before their suicide, Adolf and Eva shook hands with bunker employees. Wearing new wedding-ring and turquoise dress, a newly-minted Mrs. Hitler bestowed her coat on "Traudl" Junge, loyal secretary. The following afternoon, Adolf shot himself, and his bride took a poison pill."

Bears lap the story up.

So do you, Emil. Why is that?

Cold and wet, they pose for the birdie—adjacent to the parking lot. You use many angles for the waste ground scene, of the bunker entrance sealed.

'Fur coat finale,' is your caption for the slides.

You believe the parents will approve.

Before collecting all travellers for the yellow bus, like Christiane you—unbelievably—divulge your own dark corner. Not on the itinerary, but furries have no choice.

Trusting is very difficult, you explain. Barry and his wife Linda showed you the way. In forgiveness, you promised to carve them a Romanian bed but did not deliver. In fact, the Rileys must wonder who it was they knew. Part human, part monster, so unforgiving.

Truth is, you torment yourself about them—pretend you do not care. White suburbanites in uniformity, an anesthesia not unlike your own, except they're *other*. People who masturbate to 'foreign,' as you once did. You think friendship's something better.

The bears…well, they don't disagree.

You hurl them on the bus in threes and fours on the upper deck.

"Look at my Romania," you say. "Romanians don't trust anyone. I can't even trust Christiane or my brother Adrian. In Canada, with Diewick's, the Rileys, Linn, Ios and Fernando, I tried to overcome it. The Ceauşescus robbed their own country, and my father and mother sent me packing. In 1989, when our leader Nicolae and his wife were being executed for crimes against the state, I was on a train to Berlin. Flew to Toronto. I was seventeen."

Our driver pulls way from Wilhelmstrasse.

The teddy-bears look ahead.

Your fat-cat parents Fabrizio Benedetti-Toc and Sylvie wished you spared the bloody aftermath of revolution, and stirrings of democracy. You could make one-door wall dressers and 'Harmony' corner tables, unsupervised.

Your gift—handsel—to Canada.

A privileged first son who would make it in the New World.

People betray—the Diewick, Linn and Riley way—and what happens when our fathers do, "first couples," dictators, kings and queens? People tolerate or execute. No forgiveness. No pardon. A blind eye suffices.

"The dark corner is an ally," you tell the bears. "Our place of lies and self-deception."

Forgiveness, you do not possess it, Emil. Have never forgiven Diewick's, the Rileys, Linn, or anyone else. Your brother Adrian. Never will. Christiane Bucur.

Eyes transfixed, the teddies ignore Potsdamer Platz, and the lofty Sony Centre Cupola of many sails. As windy as any Emil Benedetti-Toc.

"My soul is Romania!" you scream to the upper-deck mites. You scream it repeatedly, like a paper tiger, wondering what it means. You doubt you have a soul to speak of. Only memory breathes fire in you.

Your nationalism stinks, my ruthless friend.

At the *Statoper* in Unter den Linden, you hand out 'Travelling Teddy' calling cards. *Visitenkarten.* On the reverse, a picture of Hugo Reinhold's famous statue: intrigued ape holding human skull.

"Text me often!" you sing-song to the bears.

Harry, the bus owner, thinks that cards are morale boosters for his clientele. The bronze chimp, like Rodin's 'Thinker,' taking stock of Man.

I know better, Emil.

You're planning to mail me, too. Aren't you? It's why you gave me a card. I remind you of traitors; those who say 'goodbye' first. To ease our own farewell, you've brought your yellow bus to the opera house. Distracting us with China's classic 'Journey to the West.' Tale of another monkey—king—travelling in search of enlightenment.

What on earth does anyone come home with, if not an ape? Hopelessness? Victory? Lost face?

Ship me with the rest, Emil: you to Viscri, me to Toronto.

Your landlord will sit me on that 'Harmony' table in a corner of the room. Your Parkdale apartment above the laundromat. From such Canadian heights, and until the rent is due, I will gaze at plywood models on your shelf. Of one-door wall dressers, four-posters, a harvest table. Doll's house chairs.

I'll watch—picture you in Viscri. Under trees some sunlit day, trying to recall pesky Eminescu lines.

One of us a chimpanzee.

You or me—arches waiting for a foot-kiss:

You live in your sphere's narrowness
And luck rules over you—
But in my steady world I feel
Eternal, cold and true!

Along with you, Emil, I hear the deafening litany…a rousing… "Betrayal is a part of friendship," "I decide who does what!" Your father, Fabrizio, in Viscri—always the loudest, is he not?—"In Canada you will find your feet."

Are you dancing tiptoe? Blushing soles. Tripping into Canada and—whoa!—it's not there. "Canada"—blank page, a *middle* kingdom—is wherever you want it, Emil. In Viscri, where everything will turn out right? No treacherous friends or lovers, malicious boss?

On your heels yet? No can do?

Dream on, Emil.

You talk about a carpentry job at the Timişoara branch of Nord Prin where your younger brother, Paolo, works; woodworking contracts with Mihai Eminescu Trust. How 'gay' was decriminalized in Romania in 2002. That there's HBO, Showtime, and Bravo on cable in Viscri. Diesel Café in Cluj. Another "Canada." You spout the Communist drivel about living well on small means—and not demanding more. As if you, or anyone, could swallow that.

It's okay, Emil, this is your style. To run. Discard. Send others, or yourself, to *anywhere but here*.

Those cruel eyes. Your dreadful verse:

You turn your back—I, mine.

What I see is only ever you?

Cut the crap, my friend.

Build on the wind, as Romania's poet says, if you must. Listen to the voices that keep you *émigré*.

BIRD ON A HIGH BRANCH

"I marvel that men seek fish where only treetops are."

All Men Are Brothers (*Shui Hu Zhuan*/«水浒传»)
Shi Nai'an and Luo Guanzhong.
(Trans. Pearl Buck)

I

"In The Second Month Of The Fourth Year Of Established Calm An Earthquake Struck"

Three Kingdoms (Sanguo Yanyi/ «三国演义»)
Luo Guanzhong

The burgundy pump.

Stiletto heel—from a foggy sedan on Gongti Beilu, one August afternoon.

He did not often see that.

There.

A limousine. The snug, ample thigh. Wang Jing glimpsed the flesh, and shied away. Thrust his shoulder against the chute cackling cement footings into new, straw-laden ground at Gong San Plaza—'A Complex Area Between Workers Stadium and San Li Tun,' as the glossy hoardings put it. At this site perimeter, far and near, where the shoe stepped out. 'Drunk in the last minute, then meeting. Tel: 588 8888.'

In a trice, it happened.

This burgundy pump; a Beijing leg up-righting itself.

"Look out, Wang Jing!" *Xiao xin!* 小心!

The rest, a devastating collision as, spiralling just above him, two umber girders—hoisted by adjacent cranes—glanced off one another. *Ch'u pi – ju pi*; like a split brushstroke. A disloyalty dance that severed crucial wires and sprang its load, bent-bastard barrelling toward earth. *Whshh. Chkk.* Where

Wang Jing stared distractedly, alongside bulldozer and backhoe, cursing. About to fill a hole.

"'Let's pretend these people are animals…'" Li Fan recited, in her Shanghai way, flushing, haughty, all amateur surprise. A half-dozen students tittered, perched behind yellow desks at Teahouse Corner in Liu Hebei village. "'… and each shoot arrows into the sky.'"

In the commune school that day, nothing was funnier.

Li Fan grinned too—as much because her first day's lesson went so well: *Zhao's Orphan (Zhao Shi Gu Er/*《赵氏孤儿》), the ancient text she quoted. Chapter-one title scratched on a board, 'Remonstration in the Peach Garden.'

Li Fan was twenty years old—a recent graduate, serious and keen, with slender hands, glossy hair, and barely discernible lisp. A French Concession landlord's daughter.

Wang Jing was sixteen, the only son of Xingtai soybean farmers.

"What does 'remonstration' mean?" she asked.

Who knew?

He observed her peachy breasts.

Wang Jing did not discover what lay beyond those opening scenes—the 'Crimson Cloud Tower over a terrace,' 'scent wafting for miles around'— dictated, repeated, inscribed in chalk, at single-story Teahouse Corner, over six weeks.

He failed to understand Chuang-tzu's 'Parable of Prince Hui's Cook' (of Tuesday and Friday mornings), and never fathomed Li Fan's handwritten posters of Luo Guanzhong's *Three Kingdoms* on "our wall": *Sanguo Yanyi/*《三国演义》.

In forty-odd years in Beijing, wifeless as he was, he occasionally pondered these mysteries but could not solve them. In the loneliest spells—and there were many for such a shamefaced, hardworking man, 'parallel citizen,' a legal and not-legal migrant, paying his own protection—he would recite verbatim the *Orphan* passages, the story of a kitchen blade, and titles that once hung beside a window. In those and the *Zhao Shi Gu Er* recitations, his voice became assured; as though he sang a favoured melody. 赵氏孤儿

This false start in life, its crevices.

How many times you could utter 'remonstration.'

Here.

Where no-one bothered much with Wang Jing. A careworn man in hiding; without women, family, or friends beyond a construction site. A muttering man who never returned to his village, Liu Hebei.

Zhao Shi Gu Er / «赵氏孤儿» / *Zhao's Orphan*
Chapter One
'Remonstration in the Peach Garden'

"It is said that Duke Ling of the State of Jin during the Warring States Period, who came to the throne as a child, was a petulant youngster of unstable temperament. But, fortunately for his realm, the influence of his benign forbears, dukes Wen and Xiang, still lingered, and the people were content and industrious."

"This is the 'nail-headed rat-tail,'" Li Fan would say, forming the stroke. "*You* draw one."

Heavy-pawed Wang Jing followed.

"That's more the 'unravelled hemp rope.' Try again."

For hours into the night they created line on scraps of paper—and, in hushed voices, talked of threaded shapes, and dots, as though their lives depended on it.

"These are 'horses' teeth.'"

Everything became lines, that April 1966. Spoken out loud in the mildewed classroom. Li Fan's drawing beneath the kerosene lamp when, at 8:00 p.m., the electricity shut off. Lines in the corners of his eyes. Lines his sentimental Uncle Jia fed him…about Jing's family in Xingtai.

"Where are your parents, Snail?" she asked, using part of his nickname (Thickhead Snail), fearing they perished in the famine six years before.

"Neighbours are still searching for them," he said, gazing into the table, at 'dragon veins'—though he did not know them as that.

March had been a month of earthquake—and suicides of high-ranking government officials in the capital, two hundred miles north.

"Shaking the four seas, shaking the five continents," his uncle said. Jia's phrase for any upheaval. A short-tempered man—known as Short-Arse Jia—who, as commune leader, housed refugees, as well as his relatives, fleeing the Xingtai destruction. "Eight thousand lives lost," he would say. At night he paced the courtyard. Added it up. "A thousand fingers eating daily."

"I hope your mother and father are found," said Li Fan, tailing off 'bundles of brushwood.'

She touched his forearm.

"A month," he replied, acknowledging her sweep across the page. One day like three autumns.

Fingertip through down.

"There is always *jihui*," she reminded him. 机会.

A chance? Not really, he thought.

Snail knew what he knew.

Uncle Jia would eventually say.

Zhao Shi Gu Er /《赵氏孤儿》/ *Zhao's Orphan*
Chapter One
'Remonstration in the Peach Garden'

"As the years went by and Duke Ling attained manhood, his nature became even more depraved, his extravagance knew no bounds, and he plundered the people mercilessly to pay for an orgy of constructing palaces and pleasure domes. He held human life in complete disregard; if anything, no matter how slight, irritated him, he would unleash a whirlwind of executions of innocent people."

Wang Jing slept fitfully on the schoolroom floor amongst the other evacuees—and near Li Fan. In the mornings, his aunt Dong Mei prepared corn cake. The group drank tea. She cooked an egg every eighth day for good fortune.

More recently, when the loudspeaker announced a call on Liu Hebei's village phone, a jumpy Wang Jing girded himself to learn nothing. Or worse. There was chatter from Beijing—and not only of General Ruiqing's leap from a third-story window. An unsuccessful suicide.

"His colleagues are laughing at him," Li Fan heard. "Our Head of State, Liu Shaoqi, told everyone, 'You have to have technique…heavy head and light feet, but he arrived *feet first*.'

Wang Jing lit the kerosene lamp in his uncle's courtyard on Crabapple Blossom Road. He took out sheaves of crumpled paper, ink. He did not want to understand this gossip or the political reasons for his uncle's meetings in Beijing. Li Fan handed him a brush—to practice 'wrinkles on a demon's face.'

In the brisk evening, early May.

"The leaders are throwing themselves out of buildings?"

"Some are," she said, a line spilling from beneath Wang Jing's nervous grip. "Deng Xiaoping said Ruiqing 'jumped like a female athlete diver…a lolly on a stick.'"

"They must be frightened," he said, thinking of his unsuspecting father and mother, silent by the unlit hearth—and how mud-brick walls could part like lips. Of trembling hands, fresh air, and dust upon his cheek. Why would anyone choose death? Or mock someone spared?

"Nice," remarked Li Fan of his strokes across the paper—avoiding further word of grisly Beijing and its hasty summoning of Party officials.

Wang Jing's face coloured.

He felt enraged by anything that moved. Save the lines of Li Fan teacher steadying him.

"Try these," she would say.

Chuang-tzu's 'Parable of Prince Hui's Cook' (of Tuesday and Friday mornings)

> *"Prince Hui's cook was cutting up a bullock. Every blow of his hand, every heave of his shoulders, every tread of his foot, every thrust of his knee, every whshh of rent flesh, every chkk of the chopper was in perfect harmony—rhythmical like the dance of the Mulberry Grove, simultaneous like the chord of the Ching Shou. 'Well done!' cried the Prince. 'Yours is skill indeed.'"*

In the lamplight, Li Fan trotted out series of 'bands dragged through the mud chopper' which brightened Wang Jing's eyes. So eager for a precise beginning, and a careful tailing off.

With close-touching dots, Li Fan soldiered across the plain.

"Rat footprints, Li *lao shi?* 李老师."

She shook her head.

"*Mi Fei* dots," Li Fan told him. "Like broken ink."

"A dot or a line?"

Wang Jing gazed at the watercourse magic.

"Neither."

"You're teasing me Li teacher."

"They help build 'dragon veins,'" she explained. "The invisible part, like breath."

Wang Jing frowned.

"It gives a painting *life*, Snail."

"I preferred 'cow hair'" he said, grabbing the brush.

"You're past that."

Lifting it back.

To and fro they struggled.

"Shanghai made you like this?"

"To behave so rudely to a man?"

"Yes."

"You're not a man."

He dashed his hand against the paper.

"Living in the French Concession made you smart?"

"I'm your elder," she said. "You ask too many questions."

Li Fan looked about—at Uncle Jia's chipped window-frame. "Settle down, Wang Jing."

Seven parts glad, three parts not, he snatched the brush.

"Let go, you freak," she said. *You bing.* Yanking it back. 有病.

He tickled her ribs, hill-valley-hill, until she squealed. Well…squeaked. "Eh, ye!" Clouds around her arms and wrists. White, pink.

Wang Jing's shadow across the table.

He kissed her lips.

Bird on a high branch—nest below.

Zhao Shi Gu Er /《赵氏孤儿》

Chapter One

'Remonstration in the Peach Garden'

"The tower commanded a panoramic view which reached to the horizon; the whole of the capital city and its inhabitants came under the gaze of the viewer from its height. Duke Ling was transported with joy to receive this unexpected gift from Tu'an Gu, and straightaway concluded that his chief bodyguard was the most devoted, loyal and capable of all his subjects."

II
"In The First Year Of Radiant Harmony Hens Were Transformed Into Roosters"

Three Kingdoms (*Sanguo Yanyi*/《三国演义》)
Luo Guanzhong

"*Xiao xin*, Wang Jing!" Look out! 小心!

The umber crane-bird of steel and cables tumbled from such height. Its wing clipped his yellow helmet, shoulder, and slammed into crawler tracks at Gong San Plaza.

"Sound the alarm!"

Pain, sudden and intense, like a nudge become a stabbing, claw. Cut down the fifty-eight year old man in seconds.

He sought an exit. An opening.

Walk, stride, he told himself.

"It needs the hospital," several co-workers agreed, running past a muddied forklift. Two Harbin men pressed rags into the base of Jing's neck. His head undone.

Only walking will matter, Wang Jing thought. I must march like in an Opening Ceremony.

"Let's get the foreman's van."

"Jing, Wang Jing?"

At this instant, a mother would recall her child; a husband, his wife. Wang Jing, blood across his throat, remembered wire.

A young woman's torn flesh.

"I know Beijing Hospital," he told his Xi'an outrigger boss. Or believed he told him. "I can walk to the hospital." Confidently, Wang Jing thought. As Li Fan strode into my uncle's village for six weeks, into the Liu Hebei schoolroom, all those years ago.

The work gang restrained him. It felt like that. Wang Jing on his feet, pushing men aside. It felt like that too.

"There are emergency rooms nearer," the company supervisor, an Urumqi migrant, told him.

"Damn you," replied Wang Jing. Did he say it?

He knew Beijing Hospital. He was going there. That was it.

I can tread in reverse, he consoled himself. To ease the spine—strengthen my heart. *Zhao's Orphan.* I will speak in Li Fan's tongue. *Zhao Shi Gu Er.* Talk her talk. 《赵氏孤儿》 Tunes in a parade. Recite lines.

I will smoke!

Protesting, the crew released him.

Wang Jing shrugged the bloody cloths. Tight.

Felt nothing.

Like a cat—from a tall tree—that regained its nerve, or filled its belly, he crept backwards, inch by inch, finding ground. His compass, fissures in a tea egg. Momentum? Slithering down like skin without joint or bone.

He'll never make it, said the faces of Gong San Plaza.

Wang Jing shuffled from the site.

Zhao Shi Gu Er / 《赵氏孤儿》
Chapter One
'Remonstration in the Peach Garden'

"Zhao Dun kowtowed before the duke's carriage. 'Your unworthy servant,' he said. 'Ventures to have something to inform you of, Your Majesty. I hope you will have the magnanimity to indulge me. I have heard that a virtuous ruler uses music to gladden the hearts of the people, while a ruler who lacks virtue uses music only to gladden his own heart. From ancient times, it has been the practice of rulers to take their pleasure either within the palace with the courtesans and servants or abroad hunting and sightseeing. Never has it been heard that an upright ruler kills people for sport. Such atrocities as setting savage mastiffs on, or shooting, harmless passersby, and dismembering a cook for some trifling misdemeanour are unheard of even for unrighteous rulers. But Your Majesty has been guilty of all these

things! If you spill blood so promiscuously, the common people will rebel and the other feudal lords will invade our state, and then the disasters attendant upon the fall of the tyrants Jie of Xia Dynasty and Zhou of the Shang Dynasty will befall Jin! It is because your humble servant cannot bear to sit by and watch the ruin of our country that I dare to risk death by speaking so bluntly. I beseech Your Majesty to turn your carriage around, return to the court and mend your ways by devoting yourself to affairs of state. No more frittering away day after day in petty pleasure-seeking, and no more taking of innocent lives! Only then will Jin be pulled back from the brink of disaster, and Your Majesty follow in the footsteps of the sage kings Yao and Shun.' Having said this, he kept kneeling in front of the duke's carriage."

(RED GUARDS SING IN UNISON):

"WHEN THE CHAIRMAN GOES PAST WAVING
COUNTLESS SUNFLOWERS BLOOM TOWARDS THE SUN"

(Wang Jing declares):

"Which way is East?"

"STEALING A REVOLUTIONARY PAIR OF IRON SOLES"

"DEEP-SEA SHIPPING NEEDS A HELMSMAN"

(Wang Jing declares):

"Which way West?"

At first light, Snail rode his Flying Pigeon bicycle to the Commune Clinic and knocked at the grating.

Kissing Li teacher was a foolish act. Later this morning, in the classroom, she would remain insulted, hurt. On his return from the capital, Uncle Jia would beat him! Li Fan, resign. Or run away. Had she filed a complaint with Lui Hebei's Party secretary? Or with Bumps on the Face who, as village barefoot doctor, right now peeped through a wooden hatch?

"Ah," said the bespectacled man, evidently from deep sleep. He waved him inside. The office no bigger than a bushel measure.

Wang Jing sniffed trouble.

"Your parents…" announced Bumps, removing his glasses.

The teenager nodded.

Gazing at moles beside the physician's nostrils.

Flared.

"I'm sorry."

Wang Jing nodded again. Fear, lead white, in his eyes.

Doctor and student faced one another across the threadbare *kwang*.

"Your *jia shushu* arrives from Beijing this afternoon," Bumps went on. 贾叔叔. "He will take you to Xingtai."

Wang Jing stared. Shook the man's hand. Memory of Li Fan—her touch, a kiss—receding with the clasp.

Tears fell across his mouth.

Father and mother were seated, that was all. A grinning brick before them.

Moles, shiny moles.

Chuang-tzu's 'Parable of Prince Hui's Cook' (of Tuesday and Friday mornings)

"'Sire,' replied the cook. 'I have always devoted myself to Tao. It is better than skill. When I first began to cut up bullocks, I saw before me simply whole bullocks. After three years' practice, I saw no more whole animals (but saw them, so to speak, in sections). And now I work with my mind and not with my eye. When my senses bid me stop, but my mind's eye urges me on, I fall back on eternal principles. I fol-

low such openings or cavities as there may be, according to the natural constitution of the animal. I do not attempt to cut through joints. Still less through large bones.'"

Outside the clinic, Wang Jing headed for the public latrines on Ten Thousand Butterflies Street.

"School's closed! School's closed!" yelled three of his friends, running by—Condor, Longface Donkey, and Eunuch. "Chairman Mao has liberated us."

Wang Jing shrugged. "*Ni ta ma de.*"

The trio came up to him—kicking his shins, wrestling their classmate.

"Fuck you," he told them again, struggling. 你他妈的.

"Long live our Great Helmsman!" shouted Longface Donkey, by far the happiest. Free from schoolroom disgrace. "Long live Chairman Mao."

"Come with us, Thickhead," said Eunuch, twisting Snail's ankle.

"Your aunt Dong Mei's giving us armbands," added Condor.

"We'll be Red Guards," Longface Donkey said.

Thickhead Snail followed all the same.

At Liu Hebei's school compound, the group halted. Li Fan and a Party official were arguing amidst some pupils.

As usual, Condor, Eunuch, and Longface Donkey had misunderstood the cadre announcement. Classes were far from ended.

"We can instruct *both* topics," Li Fan was saying heatedly. "'*Zhao's Orphan*' and '*Mao Zedong Thought*.'" *Zhao Shi Gu Er* and *Mao Zedong Sixiang Gailun.*

"These are our leader's orders," the county-level official Cheng Guangjin told her. "*Mao Zedong Sixiang Gailun.*"

"I will teach *both*," replied Li Fan. "«赵氏孤儿»and«毛泽东思想概论»."

"I'm to replace you if you don't comply."

Snail felt anguish at the sight of Li Fan. His pulse galloped like *Mi Fei* dots across a page.

Too distraught about his parents to do a moral duty, or worry about new schools and old, he would defer the apology. Rehearsed all night.

Snail turned to the soybean field—villagers bowed to their tasks. He would seek refuge in the peach orchards behind Zhang Yang's fertilizer factory.

Zhao Shi Gu Er
Chapter One
'Remonstration in the Peach Garden'

"The sight of the duke, apparently in a state of abject contrition and whimpering like a child, dispelled the towering rage that had been bursting in Zhao Dun's breast. The prime minister did not know whether to laugh or frown. He felt like a negligent father facing his wayward son; indignation and affection, shame and regret struggled within him. Then, remembering his authority, he stood in front of the Gate to the Peach Garden, resolutely barring the way for the duke."

Suddenly, Party official Cheng slapped Li Fan hard.

The insubordinate Shanghai girl staggered, and fell against the playground bucket.

Mastering the grief he felt for his family, Snail rushed to assist Li Fan —supporting her elbow.

"What are you doing?" said Cheng. "This broken shoe is a counterrevolutionary. Li Fan must change her conduct."

"'Broken shoe'?" she repeated. A prostitute?

Snail flinched.

"Are you hurt, Li Fan *lao shi?*"

Li 老师 was dusting her sleeve, and thigh.

Fingermarks along her jaw.

"I'm not hurt," she said, averting her eyes.

"You will be my instructional assistant," Cheng informed Li Fan, ushering the students, and a disgruntled Condor, Eunuch, and Longface Donkey into the premises.

Snail remained in the courtyard.

"Hurry inside, *you!*" Cheng said. "*Ni*, this is New China."

你! He indicated Wang Jing… who leapt at the man, landing punches, two, three, into his belly.

"Long live Chairman Mao!" roared Longface Donkey through the window, ripping posters from the wall.毛主席万岁!

Horrified classmates jostled for the kill.

Snail stepped backwards.

A stunned Cheng beckoned his assailant.

"Li *lao shi* is honourable," the youth said. Turning, fleeing to his uncle's house.

"Come back, delinquent child!"

"李老师 is pure!" Wang Jing shouted.

Not a soul pursued him. The gravity of his offence sealed. All face lost.

"'Death of a thousand cuts…'" he heard chanted from the school.

As he raced by Liu Hebei's latrines.

"I need to piss."

At Crabapple Blossom Road, so wishing to put matters right with Li Fan; yet alone with thoughts of his mother and father; he leaned against the crooked trunk of a cedar to await *jia shushu* from Beijing. Please never come, 贾叔叔, he thought.

"'We are Mount Tai…'" the students sang from Teahouse Corner.

Miserably, Wang Jing undid his pants.

"'We are the Great Wall…'" he steamed along.

(RED GUARDS SING IN UNISON):

"STORM FORWARD"

Chuang-tzu's 'Parable of Prince Hui's Cook' (of Tuesday and Friday mornings)

"A good cook changes his chopper once a year—because he cuts. An ordinary cook, once a month—because he hacks. But I have had this chopper nineteen years, and although I have cut up many thousand bullocks, its edge is as if fresh from the whetstone. For at the joints there are always crevices, and the edge of a chopper being without thickness, it remains only to insert that which is without thickness into such a crevice. By these means the crevice will be enlarged, and the blade will find plenty of room. It is thus that I have kept my chopper for nineteen years as though fresh from the whetstone."

III

ESTABLISHED CALM:

"Move on, old man," said the security lad, at Oakwood Residences—'A Gentleman's Private Castle,' 'Senechal of Genteelness.' Wang Jing had walked backwards past the Workers Stadium; through the narrower 'Russian' streets at the foot of Ritan Park. At the Ancient Observatory, he would turn right.

"Who said I was stopping, 傻逼?" Wang Jing glared. "*Sha bi*."

Stupid fucker.

He rested, nevertheless, beneath an electricity pylon, alongside a cluster of silver birches. Everything bordered by scaffolding from a development, Fortune Heights, that ran a city block. 'Ocean Honoured Chateau,' 'Seducing Modern and Romantic Imagination' (someone had defaced the 'S').

After pouring its remnants over his head, Wang Jing gnawed at a discarded *7Up*. The *qi xi* can fell. 七喜. His Gong San Plaza accident was far worse than he imagined. Eyes smarting, throat ablaze, a draught of fire into his brain.

He felt like two pieces.

Torn flesh.

Like a man at a cat, he reached for the place where his skull once reigned. 七喜 and more 七喜. Pulpy wetness greeted him.

At Gong San Plaza, he had not realized his head was sliced cleanly away—pitched like a softball, in one glorious arc, 七喜 -七喜 -七喜, onto a first-story girder. Landed at the foot of an astonished electrician sucking a peach.

(IN UNISON):

"RED GUARDS ARE NOT AFRAID OF HARDSHIP ON THE MARCH"

The Oakwood sentry muttered urgently into a cellphone.

Trucks lumbered in and out of Fortune Heights, welders on one knee, a bulldozer shuddering against the ground, teams of labourers manoeuvring steel mesh.

If my crown is gone, thought Wang Jing, why do I not gaze on the straw-laden mud of Gong San Plaza? Why do I have *this* view?

How have I come so far?

Beyond, like a crimson and white shoreline, the Third Ring Road bore its load.

What could a roaring overpass-traffic sing?

(IN UNISON):

"TODAY I WILL SEIZE YOU!
I'LL MAKE YOUR MUSCLES CRAMP
TAKE OFF YOUR SKIN
PLAY SOCCER WITH YOUR SKULL!"

Come off it, thought Wang Jing. Third Ring Roads cannot chant or march.

Straddling gigantically above the freeway, in murky sunlight, the half-torso of China Central Television headquarters was poised to cross eight lanes. Wires and platforms trailing from its loins like temple ware.

Wang Jing heard *people*, not engines.

What were they saying?

Amidst the din, he could not make it out.

A foreign woman strode by, her canvas tote bag in multiple languages advertising Harrow International School of Beijing, 'the brightest, bright future for every child.'

Wang Jing struggled to smile, his face wooden, as he looked up the skirts of the electricity pylon criss-crossing into the sky.

How crowds diminished. Voices grew louder and roared.

(IN UNISON):

"THE REDDEST, RED SUN IN OUR HEARTS"

Oh yes. That was it! The Mao-fanatic, comrade-in-arms, Lin Biao. Stringing adjectives together. *Zui-zui-zui*. Like no tomorrow.

Wang Jing remembered six glorious hours.

Tiananmen Square. August 18, 1966.

Suddenly the Great Helmsman appeared. Ha-ha-ha. The greatest, great day of Jing's life. Mao Zedong on that rally balcony. Parading. An hour for every second Wang Jing endured this August afternoon.

Can you hear the cheering, Li Fan?

Frenzy, joy? More people than I had ever seen.

Mao.

His simple proclamation crackling from loudspeakers and so difficult to hear above the yelling and song. His thick Hunan accent.

(SOLO):

"IMBALANCE AND HEADACHE ARE A GOOD THING"

China's leaders before us. A ribbon of men in the far distance—like your dots, Li Fan—on that wall. We believed it. We looked in that direction and saw what we saw.

You were not in Tiananmen.

Li Fan.

After my betrayal, how could you be?

(IN UNISON):

"WE PUT ON OUR BLOOD-SOAKED STRAW SANDALS"
"IRON SOLES DYE THE SEA OF FLOWERS RED"

Wang Jing stood up. The Third Ring Road with him, CCTV building in step. He would, after all, make it to the hospital.

Pushing himself backward, against posters of bunny-faced Westerners at a cocktail party, wine stacked in a connoisseur's cellar, Wang Jing proceeded toward Jianguomen Qiao, and the Dongbianmen railway station.

Last, last leg.

(IN UNISON):

"THERE'S NO GOING BACK"
"LONG STRIDES"

《赵氏孤儿》

Chapter One
'Remonstration in the Peach Garden'

"Zhao Dun had no choice but to stand aside and allow the duke and his entourage to enter the Peach Garden. His heart was full of rage and bitterness. As he watched the retreating back of Tu'an Gu, he ground his teeth, and muttered to himself, 'A blockhead of a ruler, and a doomed country—all the fault of that rascally official.'"

Two days' returned from Xingtai, and his parents' funeral, Thickhead Snail faced anarchy in Uncle Jia's village.

"You cannot be here," Longface Donkey said. "They will struggle with you like they did with Li Fan."

"Yes, he should stay," Eunuch interjected. "His uncle will clear his name."

"Travel with us to Beijing," Condor said. "Red Guards travel free."

His schoolmates' wild looks unnerved him. What had happened to his friends in a week?

"We'll see Chairman Mao!"

A glint in their eyes.

"In Tiananmen Square!"

From Teahouse Corner, you could see the hastily constructed platform by Liu Hebei's peach orchards.

Three white pointed hats of the condemned.

"No, uncle," said Thickhead Snail, pulling away from Uncle Jia's steel grip. "You can't make me do that."

"RED TEN THOUSAND YEARS!" a man, with black armband, was bellowing into a megaphone.

In spite of the hot June sun, villagers were out in force, as at Spring Festival. This afternoon, officials would denounce the latest bevy of class enemies and order them shot.

The idling lorry awaited its passengers for the execution grounds beyond the river.

"Get up there and help, Snail," his uncle said angrily. "You owe me this duty."

"*Shushu*, no," Snail remonstrated. "Please, 叔叔."

Longface Donkey, Condor, and Eunuch kicked at Snail's buttocks.

He stumbled onto the rickety stage.

"DARE TO CRITICIZE, DARE TO FIGHT"

On the raised planks, three terrified residents—with their hands tied behind their backs—stood in full sun before their neighbours.

"Grab his hair," said inquisitor Cheng Guangjin, knocking the conical hat from Zhang Yang's head—'Capitalist-roader' scrawled in chalk, on a board, at his neck.

Snail dutifully yanked the man's head.

"Eh?" screeched Cheng Guangjin, "Speak up! You didn't pay your workers for eight months. They were starving. You didn't care."

"We had no cash," replied the fertilizer-factory owner. "We paid them as soon as we could."

"Liar! Liar!" from his employees.

"You built a house, Zhang Yang."

"My wife and child needed a roof over their heads!"

"Big, fancy villa," said the man with a megaphone. "Hey? Landlord tone? What do you say, comrades?"

"Control the traitor!" Cheng Guangjin commanded Snail, tugging the youth's arm. A chunk of Zhang Yang's scalp left its home. Snail gazed at the clump. Tossed it aside.

"My wife and child will starve without me!"

"Drilling the basement, cheating his workers!" the inquisitor railed on. Cheng Guangjin guided Snail's hand to the second prisoner—the tall paper cone on her head, 'Li Fan' printed in black ink, a red cross painted through.

'Landlord's daughter, whore schoolteacher, counterrevolutionary' on the heavy board around her neck. Suspended by wire.

Snail seized her pointed hat.

"WE'RE THE RED GUARDS OF CHAIRMAN MAO"

Li Fan's head was shaved.

Always prepared, he thought. There was nothing to pull but her ear. He tried to laugh.

"Broken shoe! Broken shoe!" yelled the crowd.

"What do you say, young woman?" demanded the megaphone.

"Broken shoe," Snail prompted, shaking his head. What could he do?

"What do *you* say, Thickhead Snail?" Uncle Jia cried, beneath his nephew's feet. "Shout it out!"

Snail tilted her ashen face—a sunflower in high wind. "You have to confess."

"I AM A COW-DEVIL AND SNAKE-SPIRIT, I AM GUILTY, I AM GUILTY…"

Desperately, she tried to repeat what Snail was telling her. Bystanders mocked her lisp.

"We can't hear you!" the villagers shouted in unison.

"Th-neaky th-nake th-pirit."

"What can I do if you won't speak up?" Snail said, yanking her ear. At the nape of her neck, a crimson spot grew.

Then another.

"Bourgeois slut!"

Along the wire.

IV

RADIANT HARMONY:

"小心, Wang Jing!" *Xiao xin!*

Again? Crimson clouds. So far away? His gang mates' cries seemed to echo around Dongbianmen station.

"Duck, man!"

Shanghai passengers hurried through the gate into Beijing crowds on the esplanade.

Wang Jing peered at a woman—travelled long—as she received quiet welcome from her son, daughter-in-law, and their children.

There were many such scenes of reunion. This dragon-filled, too bright, afternoon.

The slender, greying lady, marked by the years, stood stiffly, patiently, in slacks and pink blouse as her relatives, at a cellphone, arranged the next move. Home.

From her new bicycle cart, at Wang Jing's side, a beautiful, young American was selling peach cupcakes lined-up smartly—like Red Guards, he thought—on a sheet of *China Daily*.

"Would you like one?" she enquired, pointing to the Western pastries on newspaper *Zhongguo Ribao*. Their sweet scent wafted for miles around. 《中国日报》.

Here's my new China, he told himself, gazing instead at the Shanghai woman, a nation overthrower. Her son and his wife pointed to the footbridge across Jianguomen Qiao. Without looking at them, yet contentedly enough, the elderly mother lifted her left shoulder as though raising a lifetime. The tailing-off of one particularly hard journey.

She stepped in Wang Jing's direction.

"You wouldn't like a cupcake?" asked the American, all teeth and swinging arms. "Freshly baked this morning."

"*Xiexie*," Wang Jing thought he said—thank you. He reached for what she offered, parting his lips. 谢谢.

The Shanghai arrival was upon him. How magnificent she looked in burgundy sandals, Shanghai leg in Beijing. How Li Fan. How long he could stay here, perhaps had always been here, watching the Dongbianmen gate. Grow dim.

At Gong San Plaza—six seconds, and several miles behind—his torso lay, like a branch, across muddy tracks. Head high on a first-story girder. Mouth and neck stuffed with rag.

How serenely his lady walked at the railway station.

Passing all cupcakes by.

WOULD YOU LIKE ME TO PROCTOR?

At 12:30 p.m. on Wednesday November 10th, I arrived at the council chamber. I introduced myself to Hans Kroll and to another official who had been assigned to support us. At about 12:45 p.m., we invited the 500 candidates inside. To my surprise, as we were settling the young people in and distributing documentation and the Public Service Examination, Christiane Bucur appeared, and tapped my shoulder. She seemed annoyed and informed me that the hall was "too noisy" and that she had found some applicants outside the North Gallery who thought the session was located there. I expressed surprise at this, and said I had e-mailed all the applicants about the correct location. I added that at this time of year, with so many demands on them, university students do sometimes get things confused. Although the candidates seemed to be quite normally arranging themselves, I reminded them to begin work and to keep silent. Remaining at my shoulder, Christiane Bucur stated in a loud voice, "This is a circus. Would you like me to proctor?" Not knowing what "proctor" meant, and being rather surprised by her persistence, especially in front of so many people, I asked Christiane to "back off and please leave the chamber" as she was "obstructing official proceedings."

The examination was now running smoothly and the room quiet.

When I returned to the front of the hall, I found Christiane seated in the front row. She was facing my section (not that of Hans Kroll at the other side) as though appraising the event. Overheard by the first few rows, she told me in a rude and contemptuous tone of voice that "This is a joke!" When I asked for clarification, she rather incoherently listed off, "laptops everywhere, mobile phones, earplugs, bags, coffees." I informed her that this was an open exam and that entrants were permitted everything that was being used. Indignant, she informed me that this was "not acceptable." By now, I felt that there was something very wrong about her manner and the appropriateness of her behaviour. I told her that she was harassing me, and I would like her to leave. Moreover, that she had "a nerve" showing up at all, given that earlier she had e-mailed me incorrect room location details and had not replied to my messages requesting clarification. At this, and in raised voice, she said "Well!" stood up and declared, "That silly typo" and stormed noisily out of the chamber. One would call this a "scene," and it was noted by the candidates and officials supervising. I was red-faced, and found her conduct humiliating. Any rapport with my colleagues and the young examinees was compromised. In five years at city hall, and in as much time as I have administered social and political occasions, I have never faced conduct of this nature, and certainly not in front of the general public. Moreover, my events have always run successfully.

Fifteen minutes later, Christiane Bucur came back. From the front of the hall looking up to the glass doors at the back that led to the corridor, I and two other officials could see Christiane pacing backwards and forwards, saying something, and clearly distressed. Concerned, I left the examination supervision to my colleagues and went to see if I could help. The Christiane Bucur I met in that corridor is not the Christiane Bucur I had known. She was shuddering with rage, crying, and began shouting at me, "I have come back to tell you that you're on your own." When I asked her what she meant, she told me that she had come to the chambers to, "save your ass."

By this time, and because Christiane's fury was so disproportionate to the situation, I was wondering whether to call security for assistance. Before I could act, Christiane informed me that she had "Always gone to bat for you, and no longer." I asked her to calm down. But she went on loudly and angrily, "I've defended you, covered for you."

I tried to question her about this, "Against whom or what are you defending me? What have you covered up?"

"No, no, you're on your own now. That's it!" Once again, she stormed off, witnessed by the back rows of the hall, the young people having turned around to observe this outrageous exchange.

For a second time that afternoon, humiliated, I returned to face the candidates, several of whom were concerned enough to enquire whether everything was okay.

The public examination continued without further interruption, and wrapped up properly.

Discrimination:

Christiane Bucur's inviting herself to the Public Service Examination is an unprecedented act. She is aware that I have a nervous disability and that the city offers me a medical accommodation as a result. While Christiane Bucur may have used "lost candidates" as a reason for showing-up at the examination or was verifying the room number ("silly typo"?), the fact that she offered to "proctor" the exam, installed herself in the front row of the examination room, loudly and openly criticized both me and the students, would seem more like an agenda of correction (for the disabled). While I am in favour of professional discussion about the management of official occasions, I am not in favour of being singled out or disadvantaged by a public shaming event. Whether intentional or not, her burdensome act of reproval made me feel inadequate, even incompetent, and I am neither of those things. I also note in Christiane Bucur's dealings with me by e-mail that she does not address me by name as she does Hans Kroll, that she declined to respond promptly to an urgent request for clarification about the event location, while commiserating with Hans Kroll about "a long day" when my "day" had begun at 5 a.m. that mormimg. Further, the tone of her eventual reply would seem to indicate that both Hans Kroll and I are at fault for *not ignoring* her incorrect, original message about the location of the examination! Ultimately there has been no acknowledgement from Christiane Bucur that her original e-mail to Hans Kroll, copied to me, was inaccurate. Nor has Christiane Bucur made any attempt to apologize for the roiling her mistake and subsequent silence caused me.

Harassment:

Currently, I am pursuing harassment and discrimination issues regarding the supervisor of my department, Jörg Buhs, in relation to the medical accommodation I am receiving. My belief is that he purposely, or negligently, unaccommodates the accommodation by giving me heavy, unreasonable, and insensitive assignments for my working week. As his assistant and agent, Christiane Bucur is aware of these circumstances and of the aggravated relationship I share with Herr Buhs. It is my view that in what I perceive to be the "poisoned" atmosphere that is regrettably the *Rotesrathaus* at present, fostered by Jörg Buhs, Christiane Bucur believed it was entirely acceptable to invite herself to the chamber and vocally denounce me and, in effect, the public service candidates. Her unprofessional, damning behaviour and vexatious statements caused me great offence.

Negative Environment:

Christiane Bucur's behaviour to the contrary, I am in fact a respected member of the city administration, with a considerable period of service to local government and with excellent performance reviews. The treatment Christiane Bucur afforded me at the annual November examination has caused distress to members of the department as well as to me. The Herr Buhs "reign of terror" that so many of my colleagues often mention is a reflection of the negative environment that is created by people such as Ms. Bucur acting, one assumes, with the full backing of our supervisor. Christiane Bucur's conduct, perhaps mirroring that of Herr Buhs towards me, is demeaning, bullying and unnecessary.

NECESSARY

As a result of the November incident with Christiane Bucur, I require the following actions:

1. A verbal and written apology to me and to the department from Christiane Bucur regarding her conduct.

2. A verbal and written apology to me and to the department from Jörg Buhs for allowing this egregious behaviour on Christiane Bucur's part.

3. From Herr Buhs and distributed to all departments and to Human Resources a job description of the 'supervisor's assistant' role and limits of responsibility.

4. An Opinel knife to stick in the neck of an interfering bitch who has been nothing but a cunt since she arrived at city hall.

5. An e-mail to our honourable mayor, alerting her to Christiane Bucur's fucking Herr Buhs as a career initiative.

6. Copied to our November candidates.

Adrian Benedetti-Toc
Head Clerk
Rotesrathaus, Berlin   November, 2005

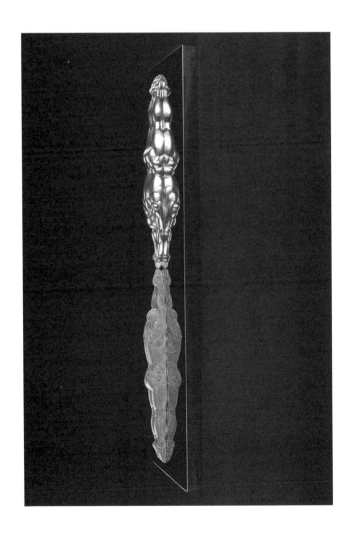

FATTY GOES TO CHINA

"Screw the imam of Niujie Mosque," said Yang Gao, dodging in and out of the city's ancient wall.

Straightforward as this August afternoon should have been—Tomasz Zaleski on an overnight express from Shanghai, Gao meeting him at a Beijing station—something was deeply wrong as the Sanlitun barber, hollow-eyed, defiant, inched stone by stone toward the Dongbianmen railway terminus.

"I'm son of Han," Gao said, coalsmoke in his rheumy glance. "I *shall* see Tomasz."

Gao peered right now, in fact, from a *Dun Tai* buttress; one of many blind angles constructed to deceive an invader. Kung Fu toes up and out, Gao springboard bounced over round-the-capital train tracks. An impossible, swaggering lightness of step. A seven foot six basketball player's leap? Chinese jumping vampire? Yao Ming! From the secret nook in a wall to this clock-faced turret above Dongbianmen railway plaza.

What on earth was going on?

How disoriented Gao felt. Last night's tears on his grimy face. No wonder, when he woke this morning, Gao found himself at eighty-one Chaonei Dajie, Beijing's dowdiest building. Fitting launch to a 'wrong part' day. Where does someone so distraught end up?

Adrift.

Even now, as he quite literally, so it felt, swooped into Waiting Hall Number One and engaged a barren couple whose newly adopted son would arrive from Shanghai. Alongside, a young Sichuan woman expecting her Chinese betrothed, sight unseen.

Lurching, soaring, was Gao a madman or ghost?

"You wait *outside*," he said helpfully, after listening to their questions and stories, "for arrivals, from anywhere, including Shanghai."

They looked about—firewagon-ready.

"We're in the wrong part of the station?"

This huddle observed him. Childless woman Sun Mee and adolescent bride Guan Dai-tai particularly gloomy, in mistaken places, about men in their lives, so they confided. As though Gao were of the same kidney; about a man in *his* life. Which was true.

Alive, dead? What am I? Crouching tiger, hidden fucking dragon.

What on earth happened to Tomasz—and to me?

"You are a student?" said Yang Gao, in Mandarin, twelve years before.

"I'm a coach," replied the German-looking customer, a couple of text-books under his arm.

Name a foreigner in Beijing who was not interpreting, teaching or colonizing something.

"I don't read, but I know how to take care of myself," Gao explained, patting the arm-rest.

Heavyset, square-jawed Tomasz "Fadi" Zaleski plonked himself in the barber's chair and laid aside his books along with a Muslim cap.

"My wife and son of course," said Gao

Tomasz looked baffled, his Chinese at a limit.

"I take care of my wife and son too," Gao emphasized. "As well as myself."

The young German nodded, glancing at a crane-bird photograph.

"And my parents," Gao concluded shyly, fastening-up his client's neck as two downy arms emerged from beneath the gown.

Tomasz tried to run fingers through knotted ringlets—then made a scissoring gesture. Westerners are the daftest lot. Snip, snip. Why else visit a hair salon? Vasectomy or triple bypass, Herr Hand Signals? Why don't you rehearse a phrase or two?

Gao adjusted the chair-support. Tomasz's head fell sharply back—parachute losing its breath, shroud lines cut. You want a Yang Gao hair-do, Porky Pie?

"You speak with Intelligent Man," Gao said in English, a language he knew inside out.

Earth to Germany.

Above the snow-white wrap, Tomasz Lazybones blushed. Nothing began like this friendship of a lifetime. Somehow the two men thrived.

For twelve years Earth circled the sun.

Then, a week ago, Tomasz hit Shanghai to fix his chin.

"*La-ilaha ella Allah.*"

You encourage a dying Muslim to say the *Shahada*. There is no God but Allah.

You wash the body of a dead Muslim.

"*Bismil-lah,*" you say, the washer. One of three. 'In the name of Allah.' Trustworthy, honest, grown-up Muslim males. You make no comment on the body.

You hold pieces of cloth.

This clean, secluded, private place.

"*Bismil-lah,*" you say again.

You lay the corpse upon a table. Remove his clothes.

Al-Ghusul. Here is washing the body of a dead Muslim.

Raise his upper body slightly.

His head.

In Gao's Sanlitun barber-shop opposite the Workers' Stadium, Gao had it all wrong about the German with a Muslim *kufie.* That quiet May morning, twelve years ago. So much for appearances and he a hairdresser.

Stout, yes. But Tomasz was an athlete, or rather a diver. An ambitious one. Twenty-eight year old diving instructor at Tsinghua University. Star hire to train the stars.

"I specialize at forward dive," he told Gao, in English. "Pike position."

"Pike?"

Tomasz shrugged, as though accustomed to the question, and the impossibility of reply, untied his gown and stepped down from the chair.

Flat on his back, effortlessly he folded his torso, legs straight up, thighs clasped tightly to his chest, forehead to shins. Toes pointed like the headdress of a bird.

Held.

Gao's habitually bored assistants stood by—then trickled into applause, commentary…and, finally, stitches.

There was no stopping this alien.

Tomasz stood and explained the diver's sole ambition: "Rip entry," as though it were a new home.

"Flawless dive into a pool," he added. "Sounds like the ripping of paper, and the water looks like it's boiling." You marveled the robust figure could model it—"no splash" he said—slipping into liquid like a blade.

Tomasz demonstrated.

"Flat hand," he said. "One palm facing the water, thumbs interlocked, fingers wrapped around the hand that'll hit the surface. Squeeze tightly, arms pressed against your head."

He raised his palm, levelled a book upon it.

"Your arms, for a head first entry, should cover your ears, see?"

Tomasz covered them.

"When you enter, every muscle should be as tensed as your arm position, so that the water can't move you."

The hairstyling delayed a full five minutes.

"I'm Muslim, from Prague, Czechoslovakia," he went on, encouraged by the trainees' reception. "I trained your Olympic divers."

Did Tomasz not have friends?

"Olympics man," whooped Gao. "Amazing."

"The students call me turkey neck," Tomasz said, jiggling the skin. "They mean it kindly."

Gao invited the client to resume his seat, wondering if he had enquired too much and triggered a party piece. The barber grimaced. Much about Gao was urgent and precise, as though hesitation, like any sideways glance, would expose him. As not entirely a boss, father, or spouse at all.

Tomasz had brought the styling to a standstill. Gao was indeed awed— but by his own head-over-heels awe...at a flabby, miracle pike on the hair-strewn floor.

Pike pause, he would later call it. May day.

So Tomasz was not German after all. European, a Czech, "living my career" as he idly put it, while the grooming chittered on. Yet pursuing his life's work in China—far from any homeland, probably unsure of what the 'living my career' bit meant exactly, apart from leaving home.

Tomasz did seem lonely. "Could you cut me like that?" he said, pointing at one of many bird photographs on Gao's shop wall.

"*Pica-pica*," he replied. "The magpie?"

Tomasz snickered. "No, that one," he said, indicating a pencil sketch taped to the mirror.

"Hm." Gao was dumbstruck that a customer might choose hairstyles from his birds. Fatty goes to China to be a Chinese crested tern, rarest species of them all?

What kind of Czech was this?

"I've never spotted that particular bird," he told Tomasz. "So it's only a drawing."

"You're an artist as well as a barber?"

The master took a clutch of Tomasz's hair and snipped, ignoring the question. Foreigners often spoke the obvious. Besides, Gao was far too excited that passions were on display.

Standing to attention, the row of aides observed.

Gao regaled his new acquaintance with the tale of Mao Zedong's 1958 war on songbirds.

"In Beijing, we beat pots and pans to keep every last sparrow on the move," Gao told him, "until they collapsed with exhaustion, like drops of rain, onto our streets."

"Why would you do such a thing?"

"Mao thought they were eating valuable grain."

"In a city?"

"His policy caused a plague of locusts the following year," Gao said. "That helped bring on a famine."

"The birds knew better than Mao," laughed Tomasz.

"Most of us knew better than Mao," he replied. "Yet we beat those kettles until we starved."

"In Prague we had giant Golem to protect us," the young man said. "Half monster, pure matter, he haunted our ghettos to protect citizens from injustice."

"So you learned diving and how to run abroad?"

"I learned from being an orphan, Mr. Yang."

Gao massaged the scalp. "Tomorrow you must come to Beijing's Summer Palace," he said. "I will show you birds on Lake Kunming."

Tomasz sniffed, as though caught off guard.

"But not looking like a crested tern, my friend."

The Czech studied his mirror, and China's rarest bird aloft.

"I'll go with the magpie," he agreed, adjusting the white gown upon his thighs. "Lop it all off will you, Mr. Yang?"

Lop? Gao nodded.

"I can be here at nine," said the diver. "Call me Fadi."

Hands clasped tightly in his lap.

"*Bismil-lah*," with a cloth about your fist, dipped in *sidr* of good-smelling lotus leaves, you press lightly the stomach of the deceased—wipe away impurities, discard the cloth. Taking up another, you clean his body.

Three times, five.

You wipe his nose and mouth—*Wudu*. At the last, you apply camphor to the cleaned flesh—remove the covering from his private parts—lay a white sheet upon the body.

Dried.

At Dongbianmen station, the Shanghai train has pulled in.

To Yang Gao's delight, the barren couple—or at least, the wife Sun Mee—and Sichuan girl Guan Dai-tai have finally understood that from *their* Waiting Hall Shanghai passengers *depart*. In haste, they descend the escalator and run outside, amongst the crowds, to greet real arrivals.

Or flee.

Wolfing his Coca-Cola, the Sanlitun barber examines a massive screen in the station concourse. Yao Ming, the seven foot six basketball player, is also drinking a *kekou kele*, but grinning.

Gao stares.

Yao Ming scores.

How riven Gao feels, desperate—like sails tangled in the rigging of a ship, beaten against ropes.

Where was his special friend Tomasz "Fadi" Zaleski?

Most weekends, Gao and he visited Fragrance Hills. They played mahjong for hours in the alley behind Gao's salon. For twelve winters, without Gao's dutiful wife and son, they toured the Bawangling forest reserve on Hainan Island. Month-long quests for the Chinese crested tern.

How do I meet you now, Fadi?

Suddenly, Gao recalls stories of the legendary Golem in Prague's alleys. Phantom defending the innocent. Never troubled about *his* chin.

"Can you hear me, Golem?" he sings into his 可口可乐 can. "Have you seen the Czech diver?"

Of course not. "I am so dead!" Gao cries, tossing aside the Coca-Cola.

"Dead drunk," says a passerby, dodging the middle-aged hairdresser.

No extravagance, no gold, silk. *Al-Kafan*. We shroud the corpse of this dead Muslim. Tie ropes around: near the top of the head, at the feet, and two for the body.

"*Al-Kafan*."

Gao had heard nothing for seven days. Surprisingly, one of Tomasz's students dropped by the barber's shop and enquired discretely about the "absent coach." Yesterday, Gao telephoned South Korean cosmetic surgeon Dr. Kyung-mo Park, at Number Nine People's Hospital in Shanghai, to ask after Tomasz and his ludicrous odyssey to "correct" his chin. 'Turkey neck' had, over the years, expanded some.

"Mr. Zaleski suffered a seizure during the operation, Mr. Yang. We could not save him."

Gao was speechless.

"His body is being held here."

"I will come immediately, doctor."

Gao was looking at the birds around his salon mirror and could not see. A bond severed—of twelve years' standing. Never had Gao received news so devastating.

"What exactly is your relationship to him, Mr. Yang?"

"There is no-one," the barber replied. "He was raised in a Czech orphanage."

"You are his employer?"

"I am his family now."

"You are Muslim?"

"I am next of kin."

"We have no record of you, or of any family here or in Prague," Dr. Park told him. "Our hospital and the embassy have been searching for a week."

"No?" he heard pots and pans near the distinguished physician.

"Mr. Zaleski identified the imam of Niujie Mosque in Beijing as kin," he said. "The imam has requested an interment in the cemetery there."

"In Xuanwu District?"

"Beijing is not my city, sir."

"Hm."

"The body will be transported from Shanghai station tomorrow afternoon."

"By train?" said Gao. "It takes twelve hours!"

"There are refrigeration facilities on board, Mr. Yang," replied the physician. "We do this by preference."

"How can I see him?" he asked, feeling bolder. "We are very close."

"The imam's delegate in Shanghai and our state counsel visited my office this morning, Mr. Yang," he said. "Mr. Zaleski's body was ritually prepared yesterday before it could be released for Beijing."

"Ritually prepared?"

"Yes."

"I would like to see him." It was as far as Gao dared go.

"You are not a Muslim, Mr. Yang, and you are in Beijing," he told the barber. "Here is a toll-free number to explain the obsequies we followed."

"I…"

"United Arab Emirates, in Mandarin."

Gao's face flushed. "Did the imam's delegate and state counsel see the body?"

"We had grossly delayed, Mr. Yang."

"Was there a post-mortem?"

Dr. Park sighed. "It was a *seizure*."

"Hm."

"Call the Niujie Mosque," the doctor said. "But I advise you that a non-Muslim cannot attend funerals."

Fearing the worst about Number Nine People's Hospital in Shanghai—and his own courage—Gao closed the handset as you might replace a bolt.

Barber Yang has found a staff entrance, and is illegally on platform four at Beijing station. Arriving Shanghai passengers bustle toward the stairs. Gao is swaying dangerously near the edge. Alongside Tomasz's train, stands a group of porters and an official—smoking cigarettes.

Gao dons a Muslim prayer cap—the one of May, that pike pause day—so large, sitting gamefully above his eyebrows. "Screw Dr. Kyung-mo Park also," he says, striding toward the front of the train. He is breathing fast. "Go-*lem* am I!"

All night in Beijing's not-so-secret underground city, accessed from Qianmen, south of Tiananmen Square—along its tunnels, past fading slogans 'Accumulate Grain'—cellphone at his ear to wife, son, and the United Arab Emirates, Gao envisaged this awful pass.

Reunited, all too briefly, with his imprudent friend.

Outside the express train's first carriage, he waves an identity card and scoots inside.

"You!" one of the railway workers yells.

Gao runs through the compartments. One after another. Tugging at one door then the next.

Reaching a baggage car, he stumbles in, and locates a refrigerated container. Lifting a heavy latch, and in the draught of chill air, he finds a blue, synthetic bag which he undoes.

A porter knocks him aside.

Gao kicks hard.

The man staggers to a shelf of parcels.

Tomasz, bound in white sheet, lies like a seahorse—and Gao reaches forward. With his razor held high.

Several employees and a supervisor burst into the coach.

Gao slashes at them—closer—lunging right and left.

"They stole from him!" he yells, until the men retreat onto platform four where an alarm now sounds.

A horde of policemen swarms the train.

Gao slams the door and rushes back to Tomasz.

"Forgive me, Fadi," he says, slicing away cotton over the belly, camphor at his nostrils. Gao wrenches apart this Muslim shroud.

Gently, he raises Tomasz's upper body.

"So."

There at the diver's groin, an encrusted smirk.

Rip entry.

Riptide.

A PARTICULAR PAIR OF LUNGS

For the umpteenth time, I poked at that bell of number five Edenhurst Grove. Suitcase and sports bag on the steps to number three, Vera Jones' house, my childhood home next door.

The Bartons' chimes were running out of juice. Peal a note or two off-key. My heart pounded and, like the wonky tune in my ears, was grim with apprehension.

"Anyone home?"

The car factory, still called Austin by locals, laboured away at my back, its paint shop fumes drifting through the jerry-built housing hereabouts. When the wind was right, I remembered, you caught the drilling of iron and steel on assembly lines. Noo-o-oozshk, cloo-o-oozshk, bynk-ga. In the dead of night too, like competing knells. Noo-o-oozshk… massive smithy-craft in the rain shadow of Lickey Ridge, a former royal hunting ground. Rose Hill, Stock Hill, Beacon Hill—its world-famous *Ordnance Survey Triangulation Point.*

Birmingham—'The Working City' as Elmdon airport had it. Central England's dole-queue hub—as the advertisements had not.

Longbridge.

Cars and trucks heaved upon the world. Ninety-four years of them. Factory hooter at 5:00 p.m.—men and youths in windbreakers, boiler-suits, scuffed shoes racing past guarded gates into Bristol Road and Longbridge Lane chockablock with flight. Ninety-four years of that too. This was my dad Frank Jones's kind of industry. And Graham Dagg's life, my stepfather, after him.

Painting by numbers.

Today though, May 1st, was more about stripping Vera's house.

The great escape.

Waiting for a reply at the Bartons, I took a good gander about. Clouds as perturbed as the hurrying workers below them. Sun-speckled, brooding. West Midlands' spring alright, last of the century. Young daffodils bordering the Bartons' path. The sloping lawn neatly trimmed. Roses fastened to attention—plant 'em, spit and polish. Front steps glistening with ruddy good health.

This pot-bellied, all too unfamiliar son at a neighbour's bell.

Rat-a-tat-tat.

Would the Bartons even come to the door?

I'd been travelling overnight from Toronto—alongside a delirious Aquascutum-wardrobed American couple, both retired high-school principals, on their way to *Shakespeare's* Warwickshire and the swans at Stratford. A twenty mile pilgrimage south of this doorstep.

I'd encouraged them to visit Cadbury World and the chimney-stippled ranges a stone's throw north of Avon's famous theatre. The other Warwickshire and Worcestershire. Staffordshire. *Black Country*—where the thirty foot coal seam made its appearance—source of the industrial revolution, bellows to the defunct Empire. I went on a bit. The sort of claptrap retired educators devour as they begin to grow. Catch up for the slowed up.

The Bard would have re-written *The Tempest* if he'd seen Birmingham, I told them. 'Longbridge, especially. Now there's a wizard's garden. The Americans' eyes lit up as though they'd unearthed a priceless Folio as my own eyes closed down on Madonna, or someone like her on the headset, after a fourth and hugely silencing Bloody Mary. 'It's a mysterious island,' I said, trying to sound like Caliban. 'Longbridge. Exile territory. River Rae running through it!' But I must have dozed off in mid-misrepresentation. Oddly, the two pedagogues had disappeared when I awoke to the landfall ding-dong.

Would the Bartons break down and give me Vera's key? I'm only Vera Jones' adopted son after all.

Across the road a dog barked.

"Mrs. Barton!" I yapped through the letterbox.

At last a silhouette appeared at the top of the door's frosted glass: Nelly Barton, chain smoker extraordinaire, Vera's neighbour of nearly forty years, friend and I suppose of late, bedside confidante.

I didn't have a chance.

Nelly—four changes of Marks and Spencer clothes a day, according to Vera—made it downstairs. She opened the door.

"Long time no see," I said.

At the end of the hallway her husband, Ted—lofty and bowed, mute to the last drop—ambled away to the seed packets in his backyard. He had once or twice spoken to me, when we arrived on Edenhurst in 1971. Just before I was sent away to Blanchland House reform school in north-east England. 'Join the Merchant Navy, lad,' he had said. (He was an Austin security guard) 'It'll make a man of you yet.' Yet? I had ignored armchair Captain Nemo, factory-gate watcher. 'Uncle' Ted was always just this. A buzzed haircut disappearing from view in the nick of time. Periscope up.

"Oh ah," said Nelly, recalling a not unpleasant chore. She was wearing a nylon housecoat and a tangerine blouse. Underneath, a pleated floral skirt that betrayed a slip. Nelly moved colourfully, a stately and unwilling mid-sixties, in stockings and emphatic peach-tone pumps. Mutton dressed as lamb, as Vera always put it when Nelly had done a favour or shared a tea and biscuit.

I waited in the gloaming of spic and span tornadoes in the Bartons' fitted carpet. A lemon, black and red convulsion. I refocused, then came to terms with the gleaming white and yellow-ochre banister that steadied the couple as they moved about their palette.

An inter-city train, the Bristol to Birmingham, hurtled past Longbridge station on its way to the city centre.

I waited.

Nelly returned at last from her through-lounge much celebrated in its day for being, amongst other things, the privilege of home*owners*, rather than council tenants, to smash down a drywall and shake hands with God. She offered Vera's house keys and the gravest of expressions.

Close up, Nelly seemed enervated. Her lips mauve-rimmed, cheeks drawn beneath the powder and blush. Sixty years or more were seeping through. Vera's demands would have accelerated them. I wondered whether she and Ted had trailed Vera's hearse in the funeral limousine my mother had arranged for herself. Or had it followed empty?

Nelly leaned against the door and sighed.

I began to speak—the first person I'd met here, apart from the cabbie, since landing at Elmdon that morning. Had she been at Vera's side through the final ordeal? It looked like it. Supervised the cremation? Wake? I assumed so, and began to thank her. But Nelly pushed the door to.

"Your mum left a shoebox on the pouffe in the front room, Enoch," she said quickly. "Nigger black."

"Beg your pardon?" I said, pressing my foot against the door-jamb.

"On the pouffe."

Wrong answer. Where Vera kicked her heels. Eighty-two years of them. Click.

Nelly Barton had had her word. Exit with a flourish. Unpursued by a bear. I guarantee the Aquascutum Americans hadn't seen anything like this in Stratford. Amongst those swans. No 'pouffe' or 'nigger black's in *that* crowd.

Like Aladdin, I watched the frosted glass as Nelly shrank away, genie-with-second-thoughts, into the brilliant white kitchen as thoroughly scrubbed, no doubt, as Nelly and number *five* ever were. Ted crossed her path. Shadows fusing.

Vanished.

Down the Grove on Longbridge Lane, an empty transporter air-braked to tackle the zebra crossing off Sunbury Road opposite the 41 bus terminus. Those unsteady pensioners fresh from the post office with another week's bingo and rent in hand. They ignored traffic.

"To the pouffe then, Mrs. Barton!" I said, somewhere between a toast and repeating directions. I glanced up Edenhurst Grove, one or two faces behind the nettings.

I wasn't surprised.

Down on Longbridge Lane, the transporter rattled into gear and towards the bridge past the Austin apprentices' clubhouse. A file of vehicles behind. Just like swans.

Enoch Jones. I'd broken every conceivable rule in the neighborhood book. Any book. I'd say it over and over again. Without remorse I'd avoided my elderly, widowed mother's funeral. Her one child a no-show. What tragedy that procession at St John the Baptist, and to Lodge Hill Cemetery. Turd, that Enoch. Always said he was a high flyer. Rotten to the core.

Know where he ended up, don't you?

All that remained of Vera Jones was simple. Emptying the house, paying final bills, and handing over the rent book to a City Council Neighborhood Office on Central Avenue. Key through the letterbox.

Closing the door of number *three* Edenhurst Grove, I paused stock still next to the miniature barometer. Setting down the suitcase, I accidentally brushed my forehead against a poster of Barcelona nailed crudely into the wall. The infamous Sagrada Familia—Gaudí's eternally sprouting cathedral.

Any minute, Vera Jones would leap from the kitchen corner, at the un-through front room door, or at the top of the stairs. You'd never catch ma sitting down. Encircled by cats, her own and several neighbours', she'd be on her feet until Graham, sideburns, Vitalis, told her to sit down

Nelly Barton had sprayed air freshener to disguise the sour milk and talc of an elderly widow's final days. Vera's slippers neatly at her armchair by the gas fire.

Handbag. Gloves on a threadbare rest.

Why would she arrange Vera's things like this? Was Nelly Barton expecting me to put them on in a moment of weakness? Want Vera back? Or was it to unnerve the reprehensible, selfish son?

'Nigger black' shoebox—and an aerosol can of 'Febreze Orchid'— lay on the pouffe. Finally, I had to remind myself, for Vera's presence was the very wallpaper, the old china has parked herself.

But if it were relief I'd been feeling, it was not cheery. Bolted to the floor, I tried to understand the ill-humored tangle that had overtaken me ever since Nelly left (another) word on our Toronto answering service. Two weeks before. Dutiful, admonishing: 'Enoch? (transatlantic throat-clearing) This is Nelly Barton in England. Your mum went into hospital last night. Unconscious, like. Poorly with her heart (another undersea throat clearing). She's in intensive care at the Queen Elizabeth. They don't think she'll be coming out again. The doctors thought you'd better know. Cheerio, Enoch.'

Exactly what had I been told? Vera was about to die. That was it. The first news, and of fatal illness, in four months. Vera wasn't expecting any deathbed scene with The Unnatural. Or much else. That's what I figured. Nevertheless, I planned to go. Then changed my mind.

I don't do duty anymore.

Every inch of these rooms was like the back of my hand. Years bursting into view as I ran my fingers over painted wallpaper.

Keep walking, I told myself.

'Get Well' cards stood upon the mantelpiece. Two of condolence—white bells, doves—on the sideboard. A chorus of people I'd never heard of.

I crept up the ladder-width staircase to Vera's bedroom. A scent of lavender powder, milk, and orchid all the stronger. Bed made up neatly, pink terylene nightie. Dressing-gown folded in readiness. Nelly's work. A bird's-eye view beyond Edenhurst Grove to the factory and Lickey Hills.

This quiet spot.

Vera must have been confined to it for weeks, months, before her journey to the hospital. Nelly Barton had spared me any warnings. On Vera's orders? Was Vera's final struggle to resist calling? Why didn't I call? Who knows? She'd pushed me beyond any limit. I, clearly, had done the same to her.

A near-empty bottle of Rose's lime cordial stood next to the bedside phone. A scrap of *Daily Mirror* with my name and Canadian number signed upon it. Cresting in the dial. The strength of a particular pair of lungs.

Felt-tip breath you couldn't miss.

ACKNOWLEDGEMENTS

I am extremely grateful to the Red Gate Gallery, its directors Brian Wallace and Liyu Yeo, staff and artists, for numerous writing-residencies and for the opportunity to live in a Beijing neighborhood. I would like to thank the community of Tuanjiehu for its significant contributions to the China segments of the book; and I am indebted to Anthony Ross and his inspired team at Opposite House (Sanlitun) for hosting a pre-publication reading. I have benefited enormously from knowing Vicki Chu, Xiao Kwang, Catherine Croll, Amanda Barry, Anne Hastie, Crystal Bell, Reg Newitt, Jayne Dyer, and Tony Scott who assisted me with life in the Middle Kingdom, and became my friends. I have been encouraged by Antanas Sileika, by editors Tammy Ho Lai-Ming, Jeff Zroback, Yeow Kai Chai, Ken Abell, by artist Sylvia Simpson, and by generous retreats at the Banff Centre for the Arts, Hawthornden Castle, the Danish Cultural Institute in Damascus, Centre d'Art Marnay (CAMAC), and Denkmalschmiede Höfgen in Grimma. My writing groups at the University of British Columbia have offered editorial insights and camaraderie. Carolina Smart and her Tightrope interns edited the book so carefully, and Jean Van Loon provided an invaluable critique of the manuscript. My long-standing friends Lorna Dunn, Marsha McDonald, Kevin Koenigs, Vivette Kady, Jim Nason, Sharon Wright, Cathy Thomson, Jim Weisz, Heather Kays, Leanne Forsythe, Sue Carroll, Michel Rice, Charles Lau, Chris Boyd, Heather Kays, and Sandra Evans are the best you could wish for. I gratefully acknowledge support from Bernard Trossman, Barry Merkley, Michael Battista and Sudaa Siva; from Zachary Morris and Kevin Wolff; from the Canada Council for the Arts, Ontario Arts Council, and Toronto Arts Council. I dedicate the collection to Ingrid and Matthias of Leipzig, Germany, for their dragon roar.

'A Beijing Minute' and 'Bird on a High Branch' were published in the *Quarterly Literary Review of Singapore* (2010, 2011). 'Four Gentlemen and a Comfort Woman' was a finalist in *The Malahat Review* 'Open Season Awards' (2012). 'Pink Virgin of KFC' and 'Fatty Goes to China' were published in Hong Kong based *Cha: An Asian Literary Journal* (2008, 2012). 'Fatty Goes to China' was shortlisted in the 2009 *Chroma* (UK) 'International Queer Writing Competition' and along with 'Four Gentlemen and A Comfort Woman' was presented at 'Open Studio' events at the Red Gate Gallery, Beijing (2009, 2011). 'Queens Take Longer, I Suppose' first appeared in *U.S. DREAMScene* (2008). 'Ducks of Berlin,' 'Sudden Memory of a Row of Beeches,' and 'Would You Like Me To Proctor?' were featured as 'A Berlin Trilogy' in the launch issue of Canada's *Oblique Quarterly* (March, 2010). 'Red Waistcoat' is a revision of 'Dog in a Red Waistcoat' (*Queen Street Quarterly*, 1999), and 'A Particular Pair of Lungs' was published as 'Pouffe' in *U.S. Blithe House Quarterly* (2003). Each story has been revised.

ARTWORK

cover: *Car Window and Plum* by Zhang Xiaogang (2010)

pg 9:   *Duel* by Wei Qingji (2007)

pg 35:   *Rosy* Clouds by Liu Qinghe (2008)

pg 53:   *Beijing Zoo* by Royston Tester (2010)

pg 87:   *Finding Evidence* by Chen Yufei (2008)

pg 117: *I–Pilgrimage* by Shi Zhongying (2007)

SOURCES

I began *Fatty Goes To China* in 1998. I have read a few books since then—and several are mentioned in the collection. I must, however, cite the following authors who have also influenced this work.

John Berger, *A Painter of Our Time* (Vintage, 1976)

Fritz Van Briesen, *The Way of the Brush: Painting Techniques of China and Japan.* (Tuttle, 1998)

Robert Henri, *The Art Spirit* (Basic Books, 2007)

Mai-mai Sze, *The Mustard Seed Garden Manual of Painting.* (Princeton/ Bollingen, 1978)

Lin Yutang, *The Importance of Living* (Morrow, 1998)

In 2012, Royston Tester became Associate Editor for Hong Kong-based *Cha: An Asian Literary Journal.* He organized the launch of *Cha* in mainland China in 2009 in Beijing. Prior to his appointment, he was a frequent contributor to the journal. His first collection of short fiction, *Summat Else* (Porcupine's Quill, 2004) is set in England, Spain, and Canada. It explores the coming-of-age of Enoch Jones. Tester's work has appeared in Asian, Canadian and U.S. journals and anthologies. Two stories, "Seriously" and "Face" were shortlisted for the 2006 CBC Literary Awards. Tester has been jury member for the Commonwealth Fiction Prize and first reader for the Writers' Union of Canada's Short Prose Competition for Developing Writers. In Canada, he has taught ESL at McMaster University, and fiction-writing at the Humber School for Writers, Toronto. In China, he has been a frequent writer-in-residence at the Red Gate Gallery, Beijing.